PRINCESS'
JOURNEY

Telham Park novels by
Jennifer Burton:

Princess' Journey

Christopher's Dilemma

Kenya's Song

Brian's Connection

Telham Park

PRINCESS'
JOURNEY

JENNIFER BURTON

ALEXZUS BOOKS

New York

Text copyright © 2012 by Jennifer Burton

ALEXZUS Books
244 Fifth Avenue
Suite B260
New York, NY 10001

The characters and events in this book are fictitious. Any similarity to real
persons, living or dead, is coincidental and not intended by the author.

Cover design by Rick Turylo

ISBN 978-0-9724733-2-3

Library of Congress number 2011909034

Printed in the United States of America

February 2012

For Princess Candice

one

Butterflies. Princess Brixton had a bad case of them. And the thought of not returning to her grandmother's house this afternoon—with a cast iron skillet sizzling up some sinfully sumptuous Southern cuisine—to attend Boravia College, an out-of-state boarding school with some rich, snobbish strangers, made her feel sick to her stomach.

Easing back onto a stack of fat pillows, she clenched the billowy down; a film in her mind playing what would be her normal routine. Adventurous, outgoing, optimistic, she is guilty as charged! But trading her straight-cut jeans and faux fur boots for a school uniform—some navy, gold and black concoction with those orthopedic-like lace-ups—was taking it a bit far. Not exactly her idea of living. Speaking of which, her not-so-perfect but comfortable life was now reduced to a mobile contraption they call a set of designer luggage. Three upright rolling cases with push-button snap locks and a name tag was no fair exchange, especially when there was no room for her laptop, iPod and other electronic devices. Well, technically, there is enough space inside but the school doesn't advocate those distractions. According to some Psychiatric Association, too much "screen time" slows the mind. Her family concurs.

The TV theme song for *Good Times*—her retro ringtone— brought her to her feet. Two text replies back to back. One was from her best friend Nadira, the secretary-of-state to be and spokesperson for drama at home and abroad. I miss you already! Safe travel. LYLAS (Love Ya Like A Sister).

The second text came from Christopher, her chocolate knight in tarnished armor, who's crazy talented with skills to cash in on. You're leaving a hole in my Soul. Sad but Proud. One Love, he wrote.

Taming the nervous fluttering, Princess fell back onto her bed, then rose sharply and pulled up the mini blinds, only to face more disappointment. *No!* The courtyard view from her fifth-floor bedroom window had vanished. Dreary, gray clouds had masked Telham Park—denying her of last-minute memories. The foggy intrusion heightened her forlorn mood, bringing on the loneliness she despised growing up an only child.

What am I doing? I don't want to go! And leave all my friends. I don't care what kind of so-called great opportunity this school is for a fifteen-year-old. I don't want to go! You think my family would know me by now.

Feel my pain. If I fake an asthma attack and scare them to death, that'll wake them up. What . . . and give Gramma a heart attack and have the guilt haunt me for the rest of my life? Cancel that. But if I starved myself—"

Switching the channel in her mind's eye, Princess could still hear Razi's jubilant cry above the roar of an excited crowd more than a year ago. She and her grandmother, whom she lived with most of the time, had just finished dinner that evening. Suddenly, out of nowhere came the wild screaming. Princess shot a nervous glance at her grandmother, dropped the dishes she had been washing, and together they rushed to the window.

Razi Pierceson, a college senior home for the weekend, was racing around the courtyard yelling joyfully, with more than a dozen boys chasing him. He was big and strong, over six-feet-seven, but he had the guileless face of a boy. Known for his signature slam-dunk, Razi was king on the basketball court. By his third trip around the courtyard, many more boys had arrived, creating the look of a mob scene.

Heads jutted out of apartment windows, curious to find the source of the ruckus. Passers-by stared quizzically. Women grabbed their children and rushed to safety in their buildings, fearing the melee.

Razi led the crowd to his building, climbed up the safety partition at the entrance, and lifted himself onto the overhead ledge. Standing straight as the hands of a clock at 0-600, he extended his arms wide like a man just emancipated and leaned forward, allowing his body to fall into the crowd of boys who eagerly caught him.

Princess remembered how the phone rang suddenly, startling her.

"You heard?" her best friend Nadira asked.

"Heard what? What?"

"Razi got drafted into the NBA!"

Princess suddenly recalled a different day, when Ms. Whitaker's blood-curdling screams echoed through the walls of the courtyard apartments. Seventeen-year-old Jamison, her youngest child, had been gunned down in front of that same building. Seven bullets ripped through him from the back, and the bullet to his brain killed him instantly. The chalky sketch of his body, drawn around a river of blood, marked the end of a young life, the result of his deep involvement in drug-dealing.

There were no witnesses to the shooting—at least none willing to come forward. After the tragedy, Ms. Whitaker, a quiet, church-going woman, was taken to the hospital from her job and then escorted home by the police. She froze as she approached the front door, contemplating the harsh reality of the scene. A mortifying scream emittted from the depths of her being, and she wailed violently for what seemed like an eternity. By some mystical force of contagion, the community grieved with her . . . and then there was silence. Ms. Whitaker was again rushed to the hospital, where she spent several days.

"You have everything together?" asked her grandmother, jolting her back to the present. "What, I scared you?"

"Sure did, Gramma."

For a sizeable woman, Arlene Brixton walked softly and could sneak up on you anywhere. "Got ya hand towels?"

"Yes."

"Toothbrushes?"

"Umm hum."

"What about the warm pajamas I bought, you packed them?"

"Yes, Gramma."

Her arms akimbo, Grandma Brixton stared at Princess' luggage with worried eyes and mumbled gloomily. Anxiety was completely out of character for the Brixton matriarch, who could put out fire with her bare hands, heal your body with medicinal herbs and predict a tragedy coming, as well as a victory. Princess had inherited that gift of clairvoyance, but she was not yet fully aware or accepting of its unique properties.

To ease her mind, Princess unzipped the suitcase. "See, Gramma," she said, pointing to each category of items.

Smiling in approval, her wrinkle-free skin glowing, she threw Princess a playful wave and walked away, leaving the aroma of her perfume in the air. "I know how you feel," she said at the door, "and Gramma loves you for trying. But it's gonna be alright. Watch what I tell you."

Springing into motion, Princess snatched her keys off the dresser and then remembered she no longer needed them. She slipped into her shoes and generously sprayed her neck and wrists with perfume. Then she fastened on her sterling silver bracelet, with its collection of personal charms, which she referred to as her 'good luck angel.' With critical detachment she evaluated her profile in the mirror while inserting sapphire stud earrings. Princess was developing from a plump little girl into a curvaceous, well-endowed teenager. *Lookin' kinda good there . . . hmmm.*

Her lively brown eyes wandered back to her pretty face. Aloe vera worked wonders at dissolving those little pimples, her fair skin radiating a pearly glow. She envisioned light streaks in her dark, long hair, no matter what her mother or father thought about it. Small compromise for sending your only child away, especially when she doesn't want to go.

"Snookie Wookie," Aunt Tikki whispered, peeping around the door. She was the younger of her grand-mother's two daughters—lively, spirited, and an optimist to her very core.

"Hey, Auntie."

The attractive professor of journalism rushed toward Princess with extended arms and gave her a big, hard kiss. "Mwah! Look at you, packed and ready. How ya doin'?"

"Not as good as you," came Princess' response admiring her well-pressed, pinstriped suit.

"You know I got to be looking good when I'm traveling. Never know who you might meet."

True to form, Aunt Tikki makes a fashion statement wherever she goes. Bless her heart. She so believes that I have all this potential 'cause I score big on all these tests, and that an education from a respected school like Boravia, coming out of the hood, could lead to great opportunities for me. I know she means well, but I don't want to go.

"You ready?" she asked.

"Um hum."

"Here, take this before I forget," she said and slid an envelope in Princess' hand with contents that amounted to one hundred dollars in crisp twenty-dollar bills.

"Thought you'd have been ready by now," said her mother walking in conservative garbed in an outfit befitting of a 'First Lady,' with the exception of the leather gloves. In a sweater and skirt ensemble with suede pumps and a matching bag she could almost be mistaken for someone's parent. Quite a departure from the tight jeans, high-heeled boots and leather jacket she donned with her girlfriends when they were club hopping. The situation's not as complicated as it may appear. Okay, well, maybe a little complicated. Princess was the favorite child between two single parents who were living their life like it's golden—since it was agreed that marriage was out of the question for them—and had not completed the mission of finding themselves and accepting parenthood. Her grandmother's house was the place of stability and comfort. It's where she called home.

"You sure you have everything?" she asked.

"Yes, I'm sure."

"Let's do this," Aunt Tikki commanded, picking up two pieces of luggage.

"WHERE ARE your glasses?" asked Grandma Brixton, running down her checklist of items as traffic had stalled along the Biltmore Parkway, the highway leading south of New York.

Oh my God! Princess leapt forward, afraid to admit that she had left them behind, but the thought of going to school without them was even worse.

"You forgot them," Aunt Tikki sensed, looking at her from the rear view mirror. "What did I tell you about being responsible?" she asked, diverting from her conversation from her headset.

Princess looked down, unresponsive, as Aunt Tikki slid over into the right lane and off the ramp.

"You have your inhaler?" asked her mother, who was sharing the back seat with her. " 'Cause you don't want that asthma to flare up and you don't have it."

Uncertain, Princess fished in her bag. "I have it."

The painful tour back home reminded Princess why she wasn't ready to leave. It wasn't a wealthy or affluent neighborhood, but its character reflected all the lives that shaped it—the common mores and ethics of multicultural interaction. The Straton Houses resembled mini-prisons, or projects, as they were more commonly called. Even in its early stage of decay, Princess' heart lay right in its corroding bosom.

When her aunt stopped the car, Princess grabbed her grandmother's keys without a word. The elevator moved much too slow for her, so she shot up the stairs as fast as she could.

"Where didn't I look?" she asked herself, rumbling through her room. She checked her closet, underneath the bed, and through the disheveled items on her desk. After searching the same places over and over, she stood still, calmed her palpitating heart beating like conga drums and whispered a prayer. It's what Grandma Brixton told her to do whenever she misplaced something. *Stand still . . . and call for it.*

A vision appeared in her mind's eye; the one place she'd hadn't looked—and sure enough, there she felt the slender wire frames, underneath her pillow, right where she'd left them.

As her aunt sped down the street, Princess texted Nadira.

Rough Departure.

two

"**R**eady," Mr. Roberts, the Supreme Steppers' leader called. Behind his dark glasses, he observed the team's lineup and pointed to Charlotte, the third girl on line, and then to Princess, who was fourth. When Charlotte turned to the left, and the tip of Sasha's nose was behind her, she stepped back, and so did Princess.

"Double time!" he charged.

Fifteen hand-slapping, foot-stomping, body-slapping girls stepped in overlapping parts, forming a percussive harmony. In stiff, precise movements their bodies made music, stepping in unison to one beat while chanting in one voice. At a ninety-five degree angle, fifteen boys stood at attention, waiting to receive their command. With mechanical exactness Princess moved beyond the rhythm *of the team, clapping her hands, smacking her shoulders, elbows and thighs with simultaneous foot movements.*

"Raggedy!" shouted Mr. Roberts.

Everyone came to a halt except Princess. She kept moving, clapping, smacking and stomping.

"It's raggedy!" he shouted again.

Still she persisted, oblivious to his instruction. Suddenly a long set of arms reached for her and began shaking her.

Startled, Princess opened her eyes. Aunt Tikki was pulling at her knee. "We're almost here, baby."

Sloped mountains, huge trees and grassy fields replaced the skyscrapers, heavy pedestrian traffic, and cement pavements of the city. Disoriented, it felt like a new day in the unfamiliar surroundings. The clouds had given way to a pale blue sky with a little sun peeping through.

Princess turned toward her mother, who was still sleeping, feeling as though she were looking at her for the last time. She was light brown and pretty, with sharp features altogether different from hers, with the exception of her thick black hair.

How could you let me go? And Dad? Seems like he would have wanted to keep me around now that all has been forgiven and we've finally come to an understanding.

"You gonna be all right?" her mother asked, drifting in and out of sleep.

"I don't have a choice."

"Mmmm," she sighed. "We're gonna miss you, ya know." Her cheeks plumped like she was trying to smile.

Why you sending me away, then? So what, I'm getting a thirty-thousand-dollar scholarship and I can meet people from all parts of the world. I don't care about that!

Princess had just been accepted as a renowned stepper in Telham Park's High School, scheduled this year for citywide competitions, and now this. Christopher had kissed her so tenderly after the party her friends threw for her. "I'm gonna miss you, Buttah," she could hear her childhood sweetheart saying. Handsome, intelligent and faster than anyone at Telham Park High, he had easily earned the nickname 'Lightning.'

Her somber mood returned, and she began thinking of ways, once again, to thwart the move. *I could pretend to get an anonymous phone call telling us the building is on fire. That'll work. Then fake a nervous breakdown. Yeah, right, and then what? Come home, be with my friends, and miss out on a once-in-a-lifetime chance? Maybe you'll like it, Auntie keeps saying. In fact, I know you will once you adjust. And one of these days—believe it or not— you'll be thanking me for the experience.*

Unexpectedly, Princess remembered the desperate cry of a new life emerging. Delivering a baby at age twelve for Mrs. Bell, a woman who lived across the hall from her grandmother, was the 'light bulb' moment. Guided by a 911-telephone operator, Princess followed the instructions to a tee when the helpless woman went into labor prematurely. The awesome wonder of childbirth far surpassed the gook and gore of delivery. As she held the warm, slippery neonate, paramedics arrived just in time to cut the umbilical cord. From that day she thought of nothing other than becoming a pediatrician.

With her head full of contradictions, Princess observed the scenic beauty of fall as the car sped along. A potpourri of colored leaves—the cypress earth, golden yellow and brick red—lay along the shoulders of the highway. She appreciated the mystique of nature, and how it abides by an invisible order season after season. Relaxed, she soon submitted to the heaviness of her eyelids and fell back asleep.

PRINCESS ARRIVED at Boravia College two hours later, just as the hourly chapel bell sounded throughout the campus, evoking a sense of slight melancholy mixed with history. An immense marble statue of Alphonse Boravia, the French immigrant for whom the school and nearby town was named, stared sternly over the open area. FOUNDED IN 1807, the granite stone monument read.

"Identification and student's name, please?" the female security guard asked in a deep smoker's voice. She was a beefy white lady wearing heavy makeup.

Nineteenth-century castle-like structures set among manicured lawns speckled with rich carrot-colored, terracotta and burnt-red leaves was hardly the look of a place you'd want to call home, especially for someone who had come from one of the biggest and certainly most popular cities in the world.

"Follow the signs that say 'Orientation,' Auntie," Princess told her. "It's that beige-colored building farther down. I remember it from before."

Inside the ornate lobby, a beautiful crystal chandelier hung from the vaulted, one-hundred-foot ceiling. Its walls were adorned with the paintings of Millet and Constant, with classical furnishings in typical nineteenth-century French style. Morning orientation had already ended, and the school tour for parents was in progress.

"You'll see each other again at lunch time," Mrs. Porter, the director of education told them as she handed Princess a welcome package and instructed her to follow two uniformed student ushers. She was a tall, thin, friendly white woman with sandy hair and a proud nose. "And we do apologize for the tight scheduling," she told them. "Normally we designate orientation hours separate from school time, but because we're admitting just five students mid-quarter, it's a bit less formal, I'm afraid."

One of the ushers was a soft-spoken white boy with brown hair and gray eyes. The taller blue-eyed blond was cocky and talkative. "We might as well warn you about the stairs," he said. "It's a hike."

The fourth-floor corridor of Davis Hall resembled a museum with its high ceilings, antique lights; marble and clay busts set on pedestals, and finely finished wooden benches.

The three stepped timidly inside the brightly lit room interrupting a literature lesson in progress.

"Do you suppose that writers expose some part of their true character through their art?" asked the petite brunette whose voice trilled with a theatrical flair, carried throughout the modern furnished space. She wasn't much taller than Princess, with a slender face devoid of any make-up.

"New admission," the taller boy said, handing her a set of forms.

"Are you Princess?" she asked, softening her demeanor.

"Yes."

"I'm Ms. Gertlant. We've been waiting for you." Clapping her hands sharply, she called for everyone's attention. "Class, listen up. I want to introduce you to our newest member of the group. Let's all make a special effort to welcome her."

Princess nodded timidly and scanned the room. There were only a few students of color—Black, Hispanic, and Asian—in the class, and many whites. Was it her imagination or were they like the coolest group of uniformed braniacs she had ever seen. Not stuffy or reserved as she had expected but then again, looks can be deceiving.

"Where you from?" asked a girl, nudging her from behind. She was so light she looked almost white, but her curly hair and the slightly thicker texture of her voice indicated she was of mixed heritage.

"New York."

"Yes! I could tell you were one of us."

"Where do you live?"

"Queens," she replied and passed Princess a miniature pack of peppermint balls.

The teacher continued questioning the students about what became clearly identifiable to Princess as Shakespeare's *Othello*. By the time Princess caught up to the rest of the class, Ms. Gertlant was asking question number seven. "What was the motive behind Othello's crime?"

"He thought his wife had betrayed him," Princess answered confidently, her voice circulating clearly throughout the room. "He had been tricked into thinking that she was being unfaithful to him, so he killed her."

"Excellent response," Ms. Gertlant praised. "I see you're familiar with the story."

"Did you get the schedule yet?" whispered the girl who sat to the left of Princess. Her big, bright eyes were shaped like pecans, and her satiny skin was golden brown.

"Not yet."

When she slid over her copy from beneath the magazine she was reading, the name on her schedule read Sherita Lawson.

"Biology's next."

Within minutes the bell rang, and Princess followed her classmates down to the third floor.

"If you want to watch us, we stream live in the studio on Thursdays," a soft-spoken girl offered. Malira had a look that could grace the cover of *Essence*, or any high-fashion magazine for that matter. She was beautiful, tall with square shoulders, and a sepia complexion.

"You're going to be living on my floor," whispered a fair-skinned, fast-talking African American wearing two afro puffs and hoop earrings who flung her arms around one of the boys in a passionate embrace.

"In Bryant Hall?"

"It's where all the freshman females live," replied another girl whose face Princess didn't see. "And where are you from?" came that question for what seemed like a zillionth time.

"Excuse, excuse." A very bold young lady said. "My name is Monique." She was hefty from head to toe with short, kinky hair. When she held out her hand to Princess, there were rings on all four fingers that glimmered attractively against her nut-brown skin. "Saw those shoes from a mile away. What size do you wear?"

"Seven and—" Princess broke off in mid-sentence as she noticed an African American boy, six feet two or better, walking toward her. He moved with a smooth, unhurried stride and carried his books in his hands, not in a backpack like the other students.

"Seven-and-a-half," she finished.

"Uh oh, he's got his eyes on you," whispered Monique.

"He does not!" Sherita said.

"What do you mean?" Princess asked, feigning disinterest.

"Oh, yeah . . . he's looking at you," another girl said between clenched teeth.

"So what!" said Sherita.

"Terry's the man, that's what," said Malira.

Princess looked at Malira inquiringly. "Terry? Why?"

"Are you kidding?" Monique remarked. "He's fine, a junior—"

"And an All-city, two-time basketball champion," Lori interrupted. "That's why."

"You gotta see him on the court," muttered Monique. "The boy is lethal."

He's coming toward me. Uh oh! Princess could see his close-cropped hair, slightly wavy on the top. His chocolate skin was as smooth as the outside shell of an ice cream bar, and he was smiling.

"Hello, hello," he greeted kindly, looking over everyone and set his gaze on Princess. "How you doin'? I'm Terry."

"Her name is Princess," Sherita spoke out.

"Can she speak for herself?"

". . . Princess," she said, chuckling.

"Well, I can already see you're that."

Echoes of "ooooohs" sounded all around her.

Meeting his gaze, she noticed his long eyelashes guarding his black, penetrating eyes.

"Your first day?"

"Yes."

"I bet you can't tell where she's from," Monique asked, challenging Terry.

"Hum . . . I don't know. She doesn't look like a Philly girl, L.A., or Chicago." He paused observing Princess from head to toe. "And judging from her style—and it's up there—I would say . . . mmm, New York."

"No way!" Sherita objected, cutting her eyes at him in disbelief. "How did you guess that?"

He shrugged easily, smiled, and said, "I'm just that good."

"You heard him," Malira said, above the moaning echoes.

"Nice meeting you, Princess," he said, and winked. "I'll see you later."

"Oh please, forget him," Sherita said. "The only thing he can do for me is hook a sistah up with Blair."

"In your dreams," Monique shot back, closing her locker door.

"I just realized something," said Malira. "Terry works for Mr. Quinn in the dean's office. All of our records are there, so he probably knew you were coming."

"And we fell for that," Monique muttered.

It didn't make any difference to Princess. Some of the boys she'd seen so far were cute, but Terry was exceptional.

THE CHAPEL bell rang at noon and all the students headed for lunch. The dining hall was a one-story limestone brick building, but the inside décor resembled any modern franchise restaurant.

Princess was hungry. She welcomed the burger, French fries and broccoli entrée with the carrot cake and cranberry juice.

"This lunch looks like it came from McCuller's," Aunt Tikki teased, referring to Telham Park's most popular restaurant. It softened the blow to see her family still there, seated and eating with other company.

"So you're Princess," said the gentleman at the table, rising to his feet. He was a small white man, precise in manner, and dapperly dressed in a dark blue suit and a red bow tie. "I'm Mr. Delmore, headmaster of Boravia."

Princess returned his handshake and quickly set her gaze elsewhere to avoid staring at the dark toupee that didn't match the brown color or the texture of his own hair. "It's nice to meet you."

"Welcome to Boravia. I've heard some wonderful things about you, and I trust your experience with us will be a worthy and enjoyable one."

"Thank you."

What a charming, soft-spoken man he is.

"Looks like your friends over there want to talk to you, Princess," her grandmother said, observing their glances. "Go ahead and eat with them."

Joining her new schoolmates distracted her anxieties. They went on non-stop, telling her about their goals and what to expect of everything from boys to school activities. According to them, more than two-thirds of the upperclassman were applying to Ivy League schools and had already been accepted to Harvard, Yale, Princeton, the University of Pennsylvania, or MIT.

THE 2:45 CHAPEL bell marked the end of the school day, and Boravians spread out throughout the campus like dandelions. Bryant Hall was a good walk from the academic buildings. From a distance, Princess could see her family standing out in front of the three-story building, awaiting her arrival. Knowing they were ready to leave, reality hit home and the butterflies in her stomach returned.

"Hey, Snook. Sho' is some fine-looking boys 'round here," her aunt teased, looking out over the grounds. "Better be careful."

"I haven't really noticed," Princess snickered.

"Hey, hey, hey, I don't wanna hear no talk about no boys," her grandmother interjected. "That's not what you came here for."

"We left your bags in your room," her mother told her.

"You've seen it. Is it nice?"

"It's cute," assured Aunt Tikki, whose opinion Princess valued. "I mean, its dormitory living, so don't expect any luxuries, but it's decent. And we met with your houseparent, too. She's waiting to meet you. Come on."

"You must be Princess," greeted the pretty, olive-brown-skinned African American woman with short, curly hair. Her skin was as smooth as a girl's.

"Yes."

"I'm Ms. Morgan, houseparent at Bryant Hall. How are you?"

"I'm good. I'm good. It's nice to meet you." Princess gazed at her with gratitude as they shook hands, happy to see someone in authority that looked like her. *She's beautiful, looks cool, mid-thirties at the most but I can tell she doesn't play.*

"Sure is a wonderful opportunity for somebody fifteen years old," her grandmother said as they walked out of the building. "But if you feel like it's something you can't handle, just say so. You can always come back home."

"This girl's not thinkin' about changing her mind. Can't you tell?" said Princess' mother to her grandmother.

She was right. There were many thoughts going through Princess' head at the moment, but going back home to Telham Park wasn't one of them. Not yet anyway.

The walk to the parking lot was more like a hike. As the Brixton's approached the car, the little family grew silent. Princess hugged and kissed her mother and they rocked from side to side in each other's embrace.

Aunt Tikki was as soft as she was strong. "I want you to do good," she said, misty-eyed, running her fingers through Princess' hair.

"I will."

She planted several kisses on Princess' cheek and forehead, quickly stepped into the car and turned the ignition on.

Princess hurried around to the other side of the car and fell into her grandmother's embrace.

"I want you to come back home a polished jewel, ya hear?"

Princess nodded, struggling valiantly against her erupting tears. After all, she was only two to three hours away and could go home any weekend she wanted. She was living on the campus of an elite boarding school with some of the brightest minds in the country. Not to mention there were enough activities and boys to be entertained for a lifetime.

As her aunt drove her family off, Princess turned away and proceeded back to the dormitory, quietly crying and brushing away the tears that streamed down her face.

three

Someone wearing Sweet Jasmine perfume led an aromatic trail into Suite 210, the last room on the east wing of the corridor. Sherita removed the velcroed pen from the door's message pad, where all the names of the occupants appeared. "Sign your name here, Princess."

Sherita opened the door to one big room divided into six personal mini-suites. Three beds were perpendicular to the wall, and three more faced them on the opposite side of the room, separated by a wide center aisle. Princess was drawn to its homey features, the warm-colored bedding ensembles, fluffy pillows, stuffed animals, and there were pictures everywhere.

"This is your closet right here," Sherita directed. "They did tell you you're going to need a lock, right?"

"She can have my old one. I don't need it," a white girl with long black hair at the far end of the room muttered.

"Well, it would be nice if you introduced yourself, Saba. This is Princess."

Saba stood up, snatching a pencil out of her mouth. "I'm sorry," she apologized. "Nice to meet you." She was a sizable girl with large, dark eyes that looked distressed. "Excuse me . . . really," she said approaching them. "I'm trying to write this paper and it like . . . sucks! But welcome anyway. Here." She handed Princess the combination lock with the number written on a piece of paper.

"Thanks," Princess chuckled. "That's real nice of you . . . and nice to meet you too."

Saba walked back to her area, then turned around and asked, "You sure you want to be here? I mean really . . . these teachers want your blood!"

"What kind of welcome is that?" Sherita smirked. "Let her at least get comfortable before you start spillin' out your complaints."

"I'm keepin' it real," Saba said, removing her uniform blouse. "These people need to get a life so they don't have to make ours so miserable."

Two other girls walked in. One was tall, blond and big-boned with a pleasant smile. The other one was a shorter, muscular, mocha-brown-skinned girl.

"You're Princess, right?" the shorter one asked.

"Yes."

"I'm Stephanie. How you doin'?"

"I'm good. Nice to—"

"Got something for you," she spoke faintly, slipping a note into Princess' hand.

"I'm Tyler." The blue-eyed girl chimed in brightly, revealing the energy behind the European accent. "Pleasure to meet you."

"Yes, you too," Princess said studying the fresh-faced girl, trying to match her accent to her geographical origin.

"They didn't tell us who was going to replace Katlin, but lucky for you, girl," Stephanie waved, looking back over her shoulder. "You've got the best seat in the house . . . 'cause everybody in the dorm knows who lives in Suite 210, and, with good reason, I might add. I'm leading the track team, Tyler's the best in volleyball, and Saba over there is the rebel. Sherita's the pretty one and—"

"Where are you from?" interrupted Tyler, who was rolling her long, blonde ponytail into a chignon.

"New York."

"What!" Stephanie's eyes stretched wildly. "I'm from Jersey." She threw her hand up in the air, meeting Princess' with a loud, smacking high-five.

Saba raised her hands high, celebrating the commonality.

"There goes your home girl over there," Stephanie pointed. "Saba's from Bensonhurst."

"Brooklyn? Git out!"

"Yeah, you know, home of the Godfather," mocked Stephanie, straining her vocal chords to emulate the deep, raspy Italian tone from the film.

"You believe her," Saba uttered. "You believe this girl?" And then she walked over to Stephanie and drew her arm back as if she were going to backhand her. "You wanna get whacked?"

Stephanie folded her upper body, pretending to be scared.

"You want a fresh one? I'll give it to you. You want one, huh?"

Laugher escaped from everyone.

"Who's that note from?" Sherita asked Princess, pointing her eyes toward her hand.

"None of ya business," Stephanie said, catching the question.

"And where are you from, Tyler?" Princess asked.

"England."

"Stop playin'! For real?"

"Bloody oh, cahn't you tell?" mimicked Stephanie.

"Yes," Tyler replied, giggling. "I'm from London."

"Are you like . . . originally from there but you've been living here in the United States or—"

"No, no, I've never lived here before."

"You mean you came all the way here . . . by yourself . . . straight from London?"

"Yep-per."

"Whoa, that is exciting."

"Yeah it really is," she smiled.

One of my suitemates is from England. Wait until I tell Nadira this!

"How do you like it here so far?" Stephanie asked, watching Princess unpack.

"It's only been a day . . . and everything's happening so fast . . . but I think I like it. Do you?"

"Ummm, depends on what day you ask."

"She loves it," Saba said flatly. "Now that she's with Damien."

"Ah . . . mind your business and concentrate on kicking that habit of yours," Stephanie shot back, and then whispered, "She smokes cigarettes like she's got a nervous condition."

Saba shrugged lamely and smoothed her hair back around her ear. "You've got Damien; I've got my smokes. It is what it is."

"Anyway, I think somebody else likes you being here, too," said Stephanie, pointing her eyes toward the note she'd given Princess.

A caramel-colored, tall, lanky girl sashayed into the room. Wearing long boxed braids and a baseball cap turned sideways, she was engrossed in a paperback novel.

"We call her Snoopy," reported Sherita.

"I told you it was a page-turner," Tyler said to Snoopy.

"Um hum."

"No, but her real name is Charity," Stephanie said. "She's the genius of the house."

"That's a pretty name. Hi, Charity," Princess said.

"How are you?" she replied, and offered up a quick glance.

At the same time a heavy thumping sounded at the door. Half-dressed, Tyler opened it.

"Is Princess here?" An attractive Asian girl with waist-length hair stood at the door with a note.

"Yes, that's me."

"I'm Tiara, hi. This is for you, from Ms. Morgan," she said and when she saw Stephanie she slipped into the room. "You were killing that girl from Ridgewood last week."

"Didn't I tell you I would?" Stephanie beamed confidently.

They slapped each other a high-five with a complicated handshake unlike any Princess had ever seen.

"See ya."

"Later."

The note read:

Your bedding supplies will be delivered to your room before the end of study period. We apologize for the delay. If you need anything else, let me know. Enjoy! And welcome again.

Tyler had changed into her two-piece karate Gi with a bright yellow belt.

"You're taking karate?" Princess asked.

"Three days a week," Tyler replied, pulling her belt sufficiently tight.

"You like it?"

"Does she like it?" interjected Stephanie. "We call her Brucetta Lee from London. Look, check this out."

Stephanie gracefully bowed, showing respect for the art, and offered up a challenge. Swiftly, she positioned herself in a cat stance, crouched down like she was ready to attack. Tyler responded with a quick defensive back stance. Eye to eye, they stared reading one another as they moved in a circular motion. With her left hand extended, Stephanie attacked with a sidekick that reached Tyler's shoulder.

Tyler responded defensively, dodging the kick and grabbing her by the ankle. She held it tight until Stephanie lost her balance and fell.

"Okay, okay, I'm sorry," Stephanie pleaded. "I'm sorry."

Extracting playful revenge and adding a little comedy to it, Tyler dragged Stephanie out into the hallway, pleading to be relased.

Okay, these girls are crazy.

STUDY PERIOD that evening was a reflective time for Princess. While digesting the day's events, reviewing the school manual, and texting Nadira in between, she repeatedly read the note given to her by Stephanie. It simply read:

> Welcome to Boravia. You need anything, holla. Hope to see you again soon. T.

The suitemates of 210 strolled in their room in tandem around 8:30pm. They dropped their books, opened the closets, plugged in curling irons and stripped down to their robes and underwear. Princess took a careful inventory of her bedding supplies. She picked up a white cotton sheet set—not exactly Egyptian 300-thread—two pillows, a brown blanket, and a thin bedspread.

Tyler helped her get set up, taking the fitted sheet out of Princess' hand, opening it out, and throwing half of it back to her. Immediately they went to work making the bed. "You can bring your own bedding from home if you want to," she told her.

"Yeah, I think I will." As Princess punched out her stiff pillows and propped them upright, she was pleasantly surprised by the soothing sounds of Karim coming from Saba's radio.

Then, in a quick turn of Saba's dial, the music switched to the fast-paced, upbeat sounds of Earth to Earth. Unpacking her clothes, Princess started to feel the groove and moved to the rhythm.

From across the room, Stephanie tuned her radio to the same station, and the music exploded in volume. Inspired by the rhythm Snoopy began dancing awkwardly and somehow turned a simple snap and bounce into jerky, rigid-like movements that Princess had never seen in a person of color. Her body skipped around, totally off the beat of the music as if she were playing around. Only she wasn't. Under the spell of the music her elbows were flapping like a chicken. Her braids flung from side to side and she threw her hands up in the air as if she were reaching for the stars.

"Uh oh, she's on a roll, y'all," Stephanie warned. "She gets like this sometimes . . . and you never see it coming."

"I-heard-that-but-you-can't-stop-me-now," uttered Snoopy in breathy, short-winded syllables.

"Calm down," Stephanie pleaded. "It's gonna be alright."

"The girl is out of control, yo," Sherita said.

Stephanie ran over and bear-hugged her, and together they fell on Snoopy's bed laughing wildly.

Saba was a rebel all right; she liked excitement. She turned on the hip-hop sounds of Unlimited Access.

"Aw, yeah!" they shouted.

"That's my jam," Sherita piped. "Turn it up."

Before Princess knew it, they were back on their feet and at it again. Freestyling around her bed, Snoopy danced as best as she could, with no shame or fear like she was the only one in the room. For Princess, all the day's events seemed hazy, like a dream: in just a matter of hours, she was in a different state, a new school, and for the first time, living in a dormitory with five suitemates.

Three hard knocks at the door brought the party to a halt. The door flew open and they all stopped cold.

"Turn it off!" ordered Ms. Morgan. "It's a school night. Lights out at 9:30."

There was still some unpacking left to do, and Princess had to take a shower. There was much to be done early the next morning, including being fitted for her uniforms at the tailor's house. The day had swept by so quickly that there was no time to record this moment that she knew somehow would be a fond memory. *Priority number one starting tomorrow: Got to write it all down in my diary.*

After the lights were out the girls listened to the soft tunes of the Quiet Storm on the radio, still talking. Before falling asleep, Saba got up and double-checked the window nearest her to make sure it was locked.

"I checked it already," Stephanie reminded her.

"Just makin' sure."

"It's still kinda warm outside," said Princess. "The breeze feels good."

"It's not the breeze she's concerned about," whispered Snoopy.

"You're from one of the toughest cities in the world and you scared of ghosts?" Stephanie said to Saba as she turned on her night lamp.

"Ghosts?" Princess asked, squinting her eyes in the dim light. "Please don't tell me there are ghosts running around here."

"No," Sherita denied. "That stupid story they're always talking about. Well, it's not exactly stupid. I mean . . . some part of it really is true. Somewhere back in the twenties or thirties, these two white boys drowned on the campus. When you drove up today, did you see the reservoir near Parker Hall?"

"Yeah, I think so."

"That's where they found them. Okay, but some people say they committed suicide because they were lovers and they were being blackmailed and if they didn't pay, they would be outed. Then other people say they had been suspected of committing some crime."

"Supposedly, but there were no—"

"Can I finish?" Sherita interjected, cutting Saba off. "Anyway, *supposedly* they had killed this guy back at home during the summer—just killed him for sport, you know how rich kids do, looking for a challenge—and when the police caught on to them they didn't want to face the music . . . and they jumped."

"It's suicide either way," Snoopy clarified.

"Not necessarily," objected Tyler. "It may have just been an accident."

"So now you have some students *claiming* to see these two strangers walking around the campus late at night," Stephanie rejoined in a hushed and mysterious tone. "And then you've got these other students saying they've seen these two white guys climbing through the dorm windows in the middle of the night—butt naked!"

"That's silly talk," remarked Tyler.

"Well, I'm not taking any chances," Saba insisted, settling underneath her comforter.

As they discussed other myths about strange occurrences, Princess grew tired and her eyelids were getting heavy. It had been a long, long day and there was no energy left to reflect. The last thing she remembered before sinking into sleep was the time on Tyler's digital clock: ten fifty-three.

four

"Twelve minutes left," announced Mr. Beekman, the math teacher, supervising a geometry exam. The soft tapping of the short, stocky man's wing-tipped shoes were as annoying as his riveting eyes gazing curiously around the room, on the lookout for cheaters. They were magnified through the thick lenses of his glasses, and could read almost anything—including your thoughts—earning him the nickname 'Binoculars.'

Which formula . . . can I use to find the perimeter of the parallelogram? Thinking, Princess glanced around the room when unexpectedly her eyes met Terry's, who was watching her from the viewing window at the door. She had not seen him since her first day at Boravia. As she drew up a quick smile her heart leapt into an unsteady rhythm and for a moment she lost focus.

Sherita watched the exchange and tossed a glowering look toward her. Princess looked the other way with total disregard to her antics, but there was no ignoring the bad vibe she was feeling for her suitemate, especially when she woke up on her fourth day at Boravia to find Sherita flipping through her notebook that she'd left on her nightstand. Sherita claimed she'd misplaced her notebook and thought it was hers. Mixed feelings of relief and disappointment filled Princess when she looked up again and Terry's face had disappeared.

After class, Princess found her way to the announce-ment board to check on the upcoming basketball events. She read: *Pre-season Scrimmage Game. Boravia Warriors vs. Wyngate Tech, Thursday Evening. Yes!* This was her chance to see Terry on the court.

"What are you reading?" Sherita asked, who had obviously been trailing her.

Princess ignored her, hoping she would vanish and faked a general interest in other things by reading over every announcement. Advertisements for the Millennium Social dominated the board, and Princess was curious about it.

"Better get ready,'cause it's soon coming," said Sherita.

"You talking to me?" Princess turned and asked.

"Yeah. That's like . . . *the* event of the year . . . so they told us. The whole school comes out, formal gowns and tuxedos . . . and the dinner-and-party thing with contests and all that . . . goes on until midnight."

"Sounds good."

"I can't wait. They say that's when you find out who's been seeing who, and maybe who's been doing who."

"Isn't that obvious already?"

"Not really, think about it. We don't have a lot of free time. It's not like being at home where you can have company, go to the mall, catch a movie or hang out in the park. We live totally separate from the guys, which I would change if I had it my way. And then look, there's no TV, computer, or video games in your room. Twenty of us have to share one phone in the hall if we don't bring our own—which will get confiscated if we're caught using them during school time—and there's only one TV room per dorm. It's like we're in prison."

"It could be worse," Princess shrugged and then bent down to pick up her backpack. She caught an ad that sparked her interest: EDITORS AND WRITERS WANTED FOR *THE BORAVIA COMMUNICATOR*.

"And it is. The weekend activities are supervised. Or you're so busy trying to catch up on some of your sleep with the late hours you keep trying to get through all the work they throw at you. So everybody does their thing undercover."

"I didn't realize—"

"And God forbid you get caught," Sherita babbled. "But you know how that goes. Where there's a will, there's a way."

"Uh huh, that's right." Princess wrote down the information and headed to her biology class.

"EVERY TIME I turn around, Terry's peeping into geometry," Malira whispered to Monique at the lunch table.

"Who's he sneaking around to see?" asked Angela, spreading mayonnaise on both sides of her tuna hero. Though she was only a freshman, she was well-endowed—extra everything. She was a year older than most of her classmates because the private school she had attended in Louisiana prohibited her from starting school before her sixth birthday.

"He's after Your Highness, right Princess?" teased Monique, hoping to pry into her thoughts.

"Um hmm," Princess responded, keeping her eyes glued to her biology notes.

"She's not paying attention to y'all," Malira pointed out, shaking up a container of chocolate milk.

Princess looked up suddenly. "Paying attention to what?"

"The *man*," said Angela, licking her fingers.

"What man?"

"You know we're talking about Terry," Sherita replied, refusing to buy her detachment.

Princess shrugged nonchalantly and continued reading.

"He's a hound dog," Sherita added.

"Meaning what?" asked Monique.

"Hounding one when he's already got one, that's what it means. His girlfriend lives in my neighborhood. I know her."

Malira turned on her serious face. "Girlfriend?"

"Yes. He's got a girl," Sherita persisted.

"Since when . . . and how do you know?" Monique challenged.

"I just told you, I know her."

Princess didn't flinch, though butterflies began some off beat two-step in the pit of her stomach. *Did I just hear her right?*

"What exactly do you know?" questioned Malira, pulling back the seal of some honey Dijon mustard. "He doesn't talk about a girlfriend and we've never seen her."

"You're not around him or in his conversation," argued Sherita.

"No, but Stephanie is," Malira shot back. You know Terry is Damien's boy. So if that was the case I *know* Stephanie would know. So what's your concern with him anyway?"

"Who said I was concerned?" Sherita replied, growing defensive. "I'm just telling you what I know."

"Yeah, well, what are we even discussing his business for?" Malira pointed out. "That's between them two."

"Yup, and speaking of the devil, look over there," Angela said.

Terry had just entered the dining hall, and his eyes scanned the place until they landed on Princess. He was coming her way.

"Want to share some of that sandwich?" Terry asked, pulling up a chair to the table.

"Sure," Princess replied, taking in the scent of his intoxicating cologne.

"Afternoon ladies, whassup?"

Responses were shallow as everyone pretended to be otherwise engaged.

"So, how's my girl doin'?"

"Good . . . if I can pass this biology test." Princess looked over at Sherita, whose eyes were fixed on them like laser beams while she scarfed down her food. *How can she eat like that in front of a guy?*

"So who's the teacher? Webster?"

"No, Cantrell."

"Whoa . . . he ain't no joke. I had him freshman year."

"How did you do?"

"B+ . . . but I worked *real* hard for it."

Princess picked up her juice container and managed to take a sip. She could feel him watching her every move.

"It's bad enough you gotta make a 95 to get an A around here, but in Cantrell's class I think an 80 average deserves an A."

"That's right," Malira agreed, sliding the salt and pepper shaker toward her.

"Excuse me," Sherita interrupted, reaching over into Princess' plate and helping herself to some of her French fries.

What does this girl think she's doing? We can eat all we want here, so why does she have to put her dirty fingers in my plate? It would be different if she was Nadira or somebody close to me, but we don't roll like that.

"I would have thought you were too busy for small-time conversation, Mr. Man," said Sherita.

"I make time for what I want to make time for," Terry responded, frowning at Sherita with a look of disgust crossing his face.

Rasheeda, Angela's best friend of eight weeks, joined them, holding a tray stacked with food. Where you saw one, there was the other. "Well, this is a change. You're sitting with us, Terry?"

"A man's gotta spread the love," he said looking at her tray, amazed. "Who you feedin', girl?"

"Me!" she squeaked, wide-eyed.

"Looks like you got enough grub there to feed a team."

Princess glanced over at Sherita. Her lips surrounded the straw of her vanilla milk shake, and her eyes were still locked on Terry.

"You comin' out to the game on Thursday?" Terry asked, quickly leaning into Princess and then backing away.

Princess stole a glance at him and nodded affirmatively. *Dag, he's fine.*

"Do that, 'cause I'm gonna play just for you."

Again, Princess nodded. *And he smells so good.*

"Looks like the right time," Terry said, looking at the short line of students.

"You're too good to stand on line?" Sherita asked.

"Not my style," he replied, rising slowly.

"Can I get you something?" he asked Princess.

"No, I'm good, thank you."

"You can pick me up one of those chocolate puddings," said Rasheeda, whose jaws were moving at high speed. "I didn't have enough room on my plate for it."

"Little girl, ain't you got enough?"

"I will when you bring me some dessert."

"Alright," he said, palming the top of Rasheeda's head and winking at Princess. "I'll get with you later, my Royal Highness."

"Oooooh," Rasheeda crooned.

"Sounds serious to me," Monique commented. "Go 'head sexy."

"Terry's a funny dude," Angela said, watching him walk away. "He had us rolling at comedy night, remember?"

"When was this?" asked Princess.

"Oh you missed it," Malira began. "They had all these activities going on the first week of school. Like an orientation to make all the freshmen feel comfortable and get to know everybody, like that."

"Uh huh."

"Anyway, they had a comedy competition and Terry got up there and did his thing. He had us rollin'."

"Well, that there wasn't any comedy act," remarked Rasheeda, looking at Princess. "He likes you, girl."

"He's just talkin'," said Princess.

"Hmmm, come on now. Don't be shy," said Malira, cocking one thin, silky eyebrow. "If he likes you, go for it."

"Even if he's got a girlfriend?" Sherita interjected, coating her salad with dressing.

"What's up with you and this girlfriend thing?" Monique asked, sounding almost annoyed. "I mean, c'mon, how much of a girlfriend can she be? He hardly ever goes home on weekends."

"Well, to my knowledge they talk all the time."

"Your knowledge doesn't count," said Rasheeda. "Especially when there's no proof."

Excuse me. Am I invisible here or what?

"Say what you want," Sherita murmured, "but I wouldn't want my man to be so friendly when I'm not around."

"He's not your man!" Malira blurted out. "So it's not about what you want."

"Sherita, focus on finding your own," Angela added, getting bored with the whole thing.

"So, what are the chances of you hookin' up with Blair?" asked Monique. "You think you can—"

"How much time do we have?" Princess asked, unable to stand the conversation any longer. She had hardly eaten a bite of her sandwich—a turkey with Swiss cheese on whole wheat. Not that she wasn't hungry, but she wanted to enjoy her food.

Sherita licked the tips of her fingers one by one, gazing venomously at Princess.

"Oh shoot, eighteen minutes," Malira realized.

"C'mon, quiz me on these questions," Princess said, and bit into her sandwich.

From: "Princess Brixton"
To: "Nadira Watford"
Subject: Boravia College

Nadira,

Greetings from Pennsylvania, home of Boravia College. Whassup, girl? Can you believe this? I can't tell you how much I miss you, my family, Telham Park and everybody. I've got so much to tell you and so little time to do it. Leaving home is like a real strange experience. Sometimes I want to laugh, then I feel like crying. It's the mornings that give me the most grief. I still don't believe I'm here, but gurrrl let me tell you . . . you have got to experience this!!!

The classes are more difficult than they are at Telham High and you've got to have a 95 average to earn an A. That's madness! And we have to study three hours each night—mandatory! Then you have your free time to study if that's not enough . . . and of course it's not. I'm in the school library right now. The technology in this school—we're talking high tech everything.

Anyway, let me tell you, this is the life. No parents. O.K., there are house parents but they're still not the real ones and they give you more freedom. Then there's crazy activities here, sports teams like we've never had in Telham Park. They've got fencing, wrestling, hockey, karate, horseback riding, bowling, golf, and chess. All of that, but they don't have a step team. Can you believe this? I was showing the girls some of our moves and they went crazy.

Speaking of the girls, the ones in my suite are mad cool. I really lucked up because three of them are black. Two are white. That's unusual here 'cause they like to spread us all out. I replaced one white girl who left and another requested a move. So we're probably the darkest suite in the school.

One of my white suitemates is from Brooklyn and she is hilarious! She's addicted to rap and is a fiend for R&B. We call her white chocolate. She keeps it real and smokes like a chimney, cigarettes that is. The other white girl is from London and she speaks with a heavy British accent. She has us crackin' up sometimes with these funny stories about working on the family farm in London and she's strong as an ox. We stay up at night, after lights out and talk about boys and dirt—mostly dirt. Our curfew is 9:30—Boo!!!

I gotta tell you I'm really feeling the brothers down here. There's only a few of them here so they're real easy to spot. And since we're on the subject, there's this dude who's the star player on the basketball team and he is *fine* and wants to go out with me. Me! Checked me out once and it was over. I had to tell somebody and since you're still my only girl. . . . Anywho, all the girls like him but he's not interested. By the way, his name is Terry. How do you think I should handle this?

Oh, and everybody loves my clothes. That is, when we get a chance to wear them. I'm always getting these stares and people whispering when I walk by. Some are hatin' but I can deal with it. (Ha!) So what's going on in Telham Park? Fill me in on all the latest developments. Give your family my love. Tell everybody I said hello. Stay strong.

LYLAS
(Love Ya Like A Sister)

five

"Watch the trend," a freckled-face, blond-haired boy in the school newspaper office argued. "You've got to look at the activity over the last twenty years. Mutual funds are the best way to go."

"My point, dude, individual stocks will outperform in the long run," countered another student. The four-eyed geek was obviously an upperclassman.

Another young man tapped his fingers on the desk, considering both arguments. "Unless you're gonna stick around for a hundred years, individual stocks tank. They're risky. Diversify, reduce your risk with mutual funds. Okay and look, it only requires minimal investment, and bonds will survive in an economic turndown."

"But they're slow and then there's fees, you gotta think global if—"

Princess chose not to break the momentum of the debate among the young men intensely examining the NASDAQ in *The Wall Street Journal* and turned away. She walked back into the foyer and read the classified section on the cluttered announcement board. Each one had been checked off except the "Science Fiction Corner" and a column opening titled, "Civic Minded."

That's not gonna work.

"Can I help you?" asked a rotund blonde with brown roots entering the office. She was short with thin spiky hair and a pretty, round face. She wasn't really old, but not young either.

"Oh, I was looking for—" Princess' voice cracked as she raised her tone. "I saw the ad posted for editors and writers for the school newspaper, and I was looking to see if there were any openings."

"Well, come on in. I'm Mrs. DeMarco, English teacher slash faculty coordinator for *The Boravia Communicator*. And you are?"

"Princess. Princess Brixton."

"This must be your first year."

"Yes, it is."

"I could have guessed it," she smiled, showing her double chin. "You haven't taken one of my classes yet. Every upperclassman takes at least one of my English classes before leaving this school."

"Actually, this is just my second week."

Her ocean blue eyes raised up above her half-glasses. "Oh, so you're one of the new enrollees."

"Uh huh."

"Wow, we don't find too many freshman interested in newspaper work. Do you have any experience?" she asked, leading Princess into her office.

"I was editor of the paper in middle school."

"Copy editing? Line editing? Layout?"

"Yes. I learned it all . . . and I used to do a column."

"Really, about what?"

The phone rang and she held up her index finger, excusing the interruption. She then tossed Princess an old issue of the school newspaper.

As Mrs. Demarco received one call after another Princess looked through the old copy of *The Boravia Communicator*. She could already see herself playing a role in its production.

"Sorry about that," Mrs. DeMarco continued, "now where were we, uh—"

"Extraordinary students. That was the subject of my column."

"Oh, right. Was this your choice to write about the top . . . well more like exceptional students?"

"Yes. I wanted to recognize young people who were doing good things . . . well, ya know, in spite of the challenging backgrounds they come from. Like the straight-A student who was discovered to be living in a car, the ninth-grader who takes care of her fours sisters and brother, works a job, her immigrant mother is disabled, yet she's the valedictorian of her class. Students like that."

"Good for you! I like that."

Princess chuckled quietly. "It turned out to be a very popular column."

"So . . . I mean . . . for the most part we're fully staffed now, but we're always in need of good proofreaders."

"Are there any news columns?" Princess asked. "Op-Ed's maybe?"

"Well, yes, Heather and Mike are covering that. They write editorials about events around campus and give their views on music, fashion . . . sometimes politics."

"I don't see anything funny in the paper," Princess pointed out.

"You mean like comic strips?"

"Well, no, more like a speak-your-mind, free expression type of thing. You know, what's the word around campus, where students share their thoughts."

"Hmm . . . has a different edge. Are you interested?"

"Very."

"How would you get your material?"

"Advertise. I could post flyers around the campus . . . do an e-mail or Twitter blast and put it in the paper."

Mrs. DeMarco leaned back into her chair and rolled her eyes from corner to corner, considering the idea.

"Anonymously," Princess added. "Positive gossip or hot tips could be first priority."

"Subject to my approval."

"Of course. And the good thing is, everyone can participate; everyone can speak out."

"Hmmm . . . You might be on to something, Princess. Let's do a mock-up, put it out there and see what kind of response we get."

THE ARMORY was Princess' third stop on the first afternoon posting her advertisements for the newspaper column. She had placed flyers in two other high-traffic areas. Anticipating a gymnasium of sorts—the likes of what she had known in Telham Park—she was impressed with the brightly lit sports arena with a seating capacity large enough to host an All-Star basketball game.

Peering inside the court, Princess had a full view of the basketball team hard at practice. Out of twelve team members she counted, there were only four African Americans, and Terry was not among them. *I'll catch him another time*, she thought and moved out into the lobby in search of the bulletin board. After careful scrutiny of all the information posted, Princess strategically placed her ad for "Small Talk" where it could be easily noticed.

"I see they got you working already," a familiar voice said.

Princess turned quickly. Up close and almost in her face stood Terry, fully uniformed, with a towel wrapped around his neck.

". . . Terry."

"Haven't seen you in a minute."

"Been busy," she said, returning to her chore.

"Me too. This is my job every day."

"Every day?"

"You wanna win, you gotta work."

"I feel you."

"Hmmm, 'Small Talk.' What's that all about?"

"A column I'm writing."

"For the school paper?"

"Yeah, you know, a what's-going-on-around-campus kinda thing."

"Ambitious, aren't we?" Terry grunted. "I'm impressed."

"I haven't done anything yet."

"I got some talk for you, but it ain't small."

"What?"

"The kinda talk that was in my note. Did you get it?"

"Oh, that was from you?"

"Like you didn't know."

Princess turned swiftly, cutting her eyes at him. "You didn't sign your name."

"I didn't have to. The letter T . . . that's my signature"

Princess ran her eyes from his muscular, hairy legs right up to his dashing eyes. "Cocky, aren't we?"

"Nah, I'm just sayin' I didn't have to because I gave it to my boy Damien to give to Stephanie, and you know that's her beau. So I figured—"

"Beau?"

"Yeah, that's what we call 'em around here. You know, your boyfriend, boo, your dude, ya dig?"

"Oh yeah, like courting. That's cute."

"One day you might consider me . . . your beau."

"Yeah, okay," Princess blushed.

"I'm just messin' with you, girl . . . but when we gonna get together, for real?"

"What's up with this?" Princess asked, pointing to a poster, changing the subject.

"The Alumni Game. That's on Founder's Day. It's like a homecoming. All the old heads come back and we hang out with them. Some of the sports alumni compete with us in the big game and it's crazy fun. So . . . gettin' back to my point. Ay, you plan on going home any time soon?"

"Not for a few weeks, why?"

" 'Cause on Saturdays we go out to the horse stable."

"Whose we?"

"My friends . . . or anybody who's interested."

"And what are we gonna do out there?"

"We gonna ride off into the sunset."

"On a horse?"

"Yeah."

"I don't think so."

"What, you don't like 'em?"

"No. I just don't see myself riding one."

"Then you need to come out with me. I'll take you for the ride of your life, girl."

Princess had to look him straight into the eyes on that one. He was smiling, almost laughing. *God, this brother is too fine!* "Yeah, okay," she said, smiling with him.

"But seriously, you'd be safe with me."

When Princess reached up to read the second page of the posted announcement, he moved in close and placed his hand around her waist. "So come check me out one of these Saturdays?"

Uh oh, watch yourself now. "I'll think about it," she said as evenly as she could, trying to sound casual.

"Come on. Give a brother a chance," he said and stepped back.

"Anything's possible."

"Good enough. I gotta git outta here. We'll talk."

"See ya."

Princess turned again as he jogged off and caught a glimpse of the back of him. *Hmmm . . . now that's what I'm talkin' about.*

Among the other announcements posted on the board was an audition for a television game show, a trip to the Grand Canyon for spring break and a bowling mix-and-mingle.

"I saw that little exchange," a female someone said from behind, intruding on her reading.

"Charity. I mean, Snoopy. Okay, which one do you want to be called?"

"Doesn't matter. As long as you call me something good," she replied. "So what was that I saw?"

"Nothin'," grinned Princess. "What are you doing here?"

"Hanging out."

Snoopy didn't appear to be as stilted and lanky in street clothes. A simple sweater and jeans outlined her feminine assets and covered her long legs. With time and maturity, Princess envisioned her walking down a fashion runway someday.

"I could watch him dunk all day long," Snoopy said.

"Who you talkin' about?" Princess had to practically yell as the noise from the court intensified.

"Terry—your beau-to-be."

"Y'all are killin' me with this 'beau' thing."

"It's part of the lingo here. Get used to it."

"Used to calling Terry my beau?"

"Yes, and the terminology, too."

"Oh snap, you got me on that one."

"It's true. He wants you, that's obvious. And he seems like a good catch, so like my mother always says, 'Hook 'em while you got the bait.' "

Princess looked at her strangely. She'd never heard talk like that coming from Snoopy. "Slow down. I gotta get to know him first."

"Okay, just giving you my psychic forecast," she continued, ogling a group of athletes standing opposite them. "And looking at him in his shorts, he's all that, some chips 'n' dip too!"

"Whatchu know about that, Snoopy?"

"Huh?" she replied, tossing Princess a naughty glance. "Deez here eyes don't miss a thang."

They leaned on each other in laughter.

"Well fix your eyes on this Alumni Game and tell me what it's all about."

"That's coming soon . . . on Founder's Day."

"Yeah, well Terry said a few words about it. But is this like an event we want to be at?"

"Definitely!"

"How do you know? It's your first year, too."

"Fall orientation. They talked about all the upcoming events and what to expect. Plus, you hear all the girls talking about it."

"Okay, I'll see. I'm trying to hang up the rest of these flyers before dinner."

"Let me help you," Snoopy offered. "I think you're gonna get a lot of feedback."

"I think so, too."

"Let's do it then."

They walked slowly, taking final glimpses at the Boravian Warriors practicing. Snoopy waved excitedly toward a crowd of boys sitting in the bleachers with an impassioned smile.

"Don't tell me you got a beau out there, too?"

"Nah. That's just someone I study with sometimes."

"Everybody studies in groups around here, I notice."

"No, well, yeah, I guess so, come to think of it. But you get more out of the work when there's more than one of you. That's why you never see me at lunch. I always eat with the Book Club crew at the Literary Hop. And since we all live on campus it makes it easier to get together and tackle the work."

The brisk wind pressed against their faces as they walked through the campus.

"You like it here?" Snoopy asked Princess.

"It's alright," she shrugged. "Do you?"

"I do now."

"What, you didn't like it at first?"

"Sure didn't," Snoopy replied, shaking her head in disapproval.

"Why?"

"I don't know. It was lonely . . . people weren't really friendly to me."

"I don't get it. Why not?"

Snoopy shrugged but said nothing further as they headed up the steps of Oxford Hall, a dorm for juniors and seniors. Once inside, Princess felt a pang of disappointment as she observed all the different announcements: college and job fairs, aviation school ads, modeling agencies and auditions for the performing arts. *Whose going be interested in my column?*

"Here, I found a spot," said Snoopy. "This person's got three modeling ads up here. I'm just gonna take one of them off." And she did just that.

They crossed over to the other side of the campus to get to the library. Pedestrian traffic was heavy.

"So who's chasing you?" Princess asked.

"Nobody, really. I have a buddy that I study with sometimes."

"Buddy got a name?"

"Well, nobody really knows him. Plays on the chess team"

"What! One of us is on the chess team? I gotta see this."

Snoopy had no comment to Princess' reaction as they went through the revolving doors of the library.

"I shouldn't be surprised," Princess continued, lowering her voice. "I saw this brother from Brooklyn on a talk show. He was the national champ. Came right out of Dekalb Tech."

"I don't know if he's champ material . . . but he's pretty good."

Inside the library, Princess had to stop and take in the magnificence of the lobby's atrium, with its black-and-white marbled floors. The open staircase was designed to encourage the eyes to follow a maze from top to bottom. On each floor the bookshelves were partitioned by glass walls and terraced by balconies.

"Look at this," Princess marveled. "The library back at my old school is just one big room."

"Wait 'til you see the stacks. They have private study rooms, lounges and—"

"Stacks?"

"That's what they call the upper floors because the shelves are stacked from one end of the floor to another . . . I guess. Look, we can post the flyers over here," Snoopy directed.

"So, do you ever play with him?" Princess asked as they left the building. "Your friend, what's his name, anyway?"

"Who?"

"Duh? Who are we talking about?"

"Oh, Langsford."

"Langsford? That's his real name?"

"Yeah, why do you ask me like that?"

"Well . . . it's not every day you meet a brother named Langsford."

"Maybe he's not a burrr-uuuther."

"Yeah, and what else would he be?" Princess sputtered a laugh.

Snoopy avoided eye contact with Princess and deliberately grew silent.

Uh oh. What did I say? No, it can't be what I'm thinking. "Wait a minute. What are you— "

"Don't go there. Just keep walking."

They both welcomed the fresh air moving swiftly out onto the grounds.

Snoopy stopped Princess and looked her squarely in the eyes. "Well, now you know. And you are the *only* one who knows."

"Okay. Alright. I got it."

"Well?"

Princess slid her gaze away from Snoopy and into the direction of the Administration Building, where staff members were leaving for the day. "Well what?"

"You know what I'm talkin' about."

Uh oh, she caught the look and eyes don't lie. "Okay, you caught me off guard with that one."

"Would you go out with one of them?"

"I don't know," Princess replied, searching her thoughts. "I could see it maybe if I grew up with one . . . okay, maybe if he was like . . . really down, ya know . . ."

"Well would you or what?"

"Okay, if you're asking me would I go out with a white dude . . . I would probably say no. But I don't know any of them, either. And I've never been approached by one."

"And if you were?"

"I mean . . . I don't know," Princess answered cautiously. "If I liked him, maybe."

"See what I mean." Snoopy sucked her teeth, rolled her eyes and turned away.

"You're really thinking about this, huh?"

"Could be headed there."

"And how does he feel?"

"Good. Like it's a natural thing."

"So what's the problem?"

Snoopy locked arms with Princess and they continued to walk. "Okay, hear me out. He asked me to be his partner . . . at the Social."

"No he didn't. And what did you say?"

"See, that's what I mean." Snoopy stopped again. "If you're reacting like this, what's everybody else gonna say?"

"Who cares what they say? These are the same people who don't give you the time of day. It's *you* that's gotta feel right with it."

Snoopy's eyes darted around the campus. "I shouldn't care 'cause it's not like anybody else asked me. But I don't want to look stupid, either."

"Stupid to who?" Princess asked. "All I can say is, you have to feel comfortable with it. And it's not like you're talking about forever with the guy."

Snoopy moved in closer to Princess. "Just don't tell anybody."

"Who am I gonna tell, and why would I?"

Snoopy put her arm around Princess and said, "I'm glad you came here."

"Hey, that's what sistazs are for."

six

"You've got to get there early if you want good seats," Stephanie repeated and headed out the door. Thursday evening's basketball game arrived quickly. Princess, Sherita, Snoopy, and Stephanie, donned in their urban sportswear, fabulous footwear and designer bags, started out together and were soon joined by Monique and Malira at the Armory.

From freshman to senior, it looked like every student on campus came to watch the Boravian Warriors play against arch rival Wyngate Tech.

"Is he really that good, Snoopy?"

"You've asked me that a thousand times, Princess. What did I tell you?" Snoopy eyeballed every strapping athlete that passed by. Supporters of Wyngate Tech were swelling in numbers. "Oh, and give me some gum."

"But is he like really good—okay, okay, no more questions."

"Oh, my God! Look at those biceps," whispered Malira, huddled between Princess and the group of girls as they moved through the crowded lobby. Members of the wrestling team came out of practice from the ring—still in their workout clothes—to see the game.

"Ain't nothin' I want," said Stephanie, completely unfazed.

"Let's get closer to Benjamin," said a thin blonde, walking among the West Coast girls. They wore tight jeans, high-heeled boots, and lots of make-up. "I want him to see me."

"Did you hear that?" Malira questioned.

"They ain't all that," Monique remarked.

"For some reason they *think* they are," Snoopy muttered, feeling a pang of envy at their audacious confidence. "Looking like Barbie Dolls."

"When did Barbie start wearing fake boobs?" commented Malira. " 'Cause I heard the two senior girls got implants."

"Where'd you hear that?" asked Monique.

"Kill all that!" Stephanie insisted. She was focused on moving inside and getting the best seats.

"One for three, two for five. Beautiful roses," said Michael, a junior from Connecticut and vice-president of the student body. The brown-eyed, dark haired six-foot student had the physical appeal of a celebrity—complete with a sweet smile, even skin and white teeth. He was wearing a jacket with the name 'True Light International' written on it.

"Ooooh, they smell like a garden," Malira noted as he passed by them.

"Gotta give it to him," commended Snoopy. "Gotta hustle for everything. Flowers one day, a calculator on key chains the next. I saw him selling tube socks one day last week—blew my mind. But I sho' did buy a pack. He's got the best deals around."

"Where does he get all that stuff?" asked Princess.

"I don't know, but remember at orientation? Oh, that's right, I forgot you weren't there. Well, when they introduced the student body president and vice-president, he told us his father had been a political prisoner in Turkey for like . . . thirteen years. It was real sad, too. He said this political group—that's the name on his shirt—saved his father's life and now he wants to help raise money to save others. Then there's all these other causes he talked about that he's trying to raise money for."

"Wow . . . a millionaire in the making," Princess said, watching him move from group to group.

Snoopy agreed. "You see it all over him."

The girls bounced to the heart-thumping rhythms of rap music playing as they entered the dazzling arena. Princess smiled inside, reverting back to childhood memories when she attended the Ice Capades at Madison Square Garden. She remembered the screaming fans, the festive music, the long streams of colored lights bouncing in circular motion along the stands, and an icy floor that seemed to stretch for miles.

"C'mon," Stephanie directed. "We're going straight down to the front." Stephanie was on a mission to best position them where she could have close access to Damien.

THE INTRODUCTION of the Boravia Warriors brought the crowd to their feet. An unexpected rush of sensation zoomed through Princess when she laid eyes on Terry's awesome body—the legs, the thighs, the shoulders—chiseled to perfection. Stephanie went wild, doing sharp, two-fingered whistles when Damien was introduced.

"Lawdy, Lawdy, Lawdy, sho is a blessing to be a Mandingo," said Monique.

"Right reckon it is, Celie," Stephanie agreed.

"I see you looking at Terry," said Sherita.

What, is she reading my thoughts now? "How do you see that? I'm looking at everybody," Princess asserted. "Is that alright with you?"

"Yeah, I know you're looking at him," Sherita contended, her tone accusatory.

"Well, I'm looking," admitted Malira, who heard the exchange. "I'm trying to see everything in sight and what I can't see, I'll just use a little imagination."

Amid the noise, they burst into laughter.

"Uh oh, here he comes," Stephanie teased, casting her eyes over toward Sherita.

Furious screams sounded out above the applause as the tall, brawny, caramel-colored athlete wearing his curly hair in a ponytail was introduced. Sherita could barely contain herself. She was on her feet, fiercely applauding and yelling out his name.

Just look at her, gooey as putty.

As the players organized the line-up, Terry broke out of the circle momentarily and made his way toward Princess' group. "Terry!" the crowd roared as he slapped hands with admiring fans.

He continued up the stairs over to Princess and reached in toward her. When she extended her hand, he gently kissed the back of it. "My good luck charm."

"Woooos" sounded out of the audience. Every eye was on Princess and then, in a hot second, with a smile and a wink, Terry was gone.

"My kinda girl, yo!" shouted Stephanie, stretching her arm over Snoopy to Princess, slapping her on the thigh. "It's on, baby!"

NINETY-SIX to ninety-four was the score, and the Warriors were down by two. The game was fiercely competitive and either team ever led by more than three points. Terry had worked hard, playing most of the game. Underneath a shower of perspiration his face was determined, his actions calculated. Twenty-two seconds remained in the fourth and the Warriors held the ball.

Damien received the pass and tossed the ball to Terry, who passed it to Ivan, who brought it to center court. He dribbled for two, three, four seconds. Then passed the ball back to Terry with ten seconds left. Terry bounced the ball three times, deftly evading his opponent. He reached in like he would shoot and skillfully maneuvered a crossover move, neatly freezing out members of the other team.

He quickly dribbled three more times, targeted the net for a three-pointer, and the ball flew out of his hands. It hit the rim, rolled completely around it and stalled. Time stopped. The noise faded to near silence as everyone held their breath.

Into the net the ball fell. Boravians jumped to their feet with explosive roars. With six seconds left and Boravia now leading by one point, Wyngate Tech called a time-out.

"They still got time to score, y'all," observed Stephanie.

"But there's only six seconds left," Snoopy argued.

"That's enough time to inbound the ball and try to get a shot off, and if it goes in—"

"That's right, and we can't foul them," added Princess.

"Well, my money's on Boravia," Snoopy declared.

"Okay y'all, here we go," signaled Stephanie.

As the final seconds raced by, one player from Wyngate Tech passed the ball to his teammate. Anticipating the inbound pass, Terry intercepted, securing the ball in mid-air, and flew ferociously down a wide-open court. As he released the ball the buzzer sounded, signaling the end of the game. The ball went in—*swoosh*—nothing but net.

Rushing to their feet, the crowd went mad. Thunderous applause celebrated the victory with screaming fans cheering and dog-like barking echoes sounding throughout the armory.

"Yes! Yes! Yes!" Princess cried, extending both arms up in the air.

"Terry's the man!" Stephanie trumpeted. "Terry-is-the-man!"

"He killed 'em, Princess!" Snoopy yelled, throwing Princess a high-five.

In seconds, Terry's face was buried among the crowd, and blue streaks of camera flashes flickered over the court. Elated teammates swarmed around, huddling and embracing him.

"C'mon Princess," Stephanie urged. "We're going to the locker room."

"I thought we weren't allowed to go near the team when—"

"You forget who you're talkin' to?" Stephanie asked, grabbing her by the hand.

Desperately curious, Sherita asked, "Where y'all going?"

"None of your business," Stephanie snapped. "This is a private matter."

OUTSIDE THE locker room the thrill of the game lingered while reporters filed inside to get an interview with the players. Stephanie was a well-regarded sports celebrity in her own right, greeting the press, coaches from other schools, and talking to other athletes.

"Whatchu doing here, girl?" Terry asked brightly as the Boravian Warriors strolled out, clean and fully dressed. Already glowing over his winning performance, his good looks were magnified.

"Came to congratulate a brother," Princess replied and hugged him warmly. "You did your thing!"

"Just taking care of business, that's all."

"You rocked 'em!" praised Stephanie, giving Terry a quick hug and running over to Damien.

"I see you smiling. Enjoyed yourself?"

"I knew you had skills," Princess nodded, "but—"

"Excuse me, mind if we get a shot of you with the Coach," a sideline reporter asked Terry, and came in between them.

"Depends on how much you're paying me," Terry joked, and pulled Princess close to him and posed.

The photographs and the constant interruptions made it almost impossible for the two to converse with one another until they made their way out of the Armory.

"Yo, yo, Mike," Terry called as they exited. He was still in the lobby selling roses. "One over here."

"Make that two," shouted Damien walking behind them.

"For the Princess," Terry said, handing her a red rose.

It was a carnival-like atmosphere outside as Boravians bombarded them with praise and adulation. Curfew hour had been extended an hour and everyone was taking advantage of it. Lines of couples hung close and the guys, including some team members, accompanied their girlfriends to their dorms.

Even as they walked up the stairs of Bryant Hall, adoring fans were constantly interrupting Terry. "Hold up," he told the group that had followed them. "Let me walk the Princess inside."

"Stop calling me 'the Princess.' People are gonna start lookin' at me."

"Too late for that; they're already lookin'," he said, pulling her closer to him. "Not the way I am, of course. Betta not be."

Princess laughed, denying her desire to look in his eyes.

Stephanie and Damien were right behind them, locked in a passionate kiss. They could almost pass as brother and sister—same complexion, similar features, and both were outstanding athletes.

" 'Preciate the walk," Princess said, stepping inside the foyer of Bryant Hall. Terry's look had grown more intense—the kind of look a guy gives to a girl when he's ready to make a move. *Please don't tell me he's gonna try to kiss me with all these people around.*

He slipped his hand into hers, leaned into her and gently kissed her right cheek. "I played just for you tonight," he whispered and stepped off. "Have a good one, Princess . . . and dream about me."

"Get outta here, Terry."

He clucked and winked, heading out the door. "See you later, girl."

Savoring the soft feel of Terry's lips on her cheek, Princess didn't just walk; she floated into her room, inhaling the rich, sweet scent of her rose.

"Where were you?" Sherita demanded, snatching the door open.

"Ah, excuse me?" Princess answered, tickling her nose with the rose. "I'm reporting to you now?"

Stephanie, who was with her, shot a questioning glance at Princess.

"I know you were with Terry," Sherita said crossly.

Reggae music sounded out of Saba's corner, who had arrived just minutes before they did. "Oooooh, I like that, turn it up," said Princess, ignoring Sherita.

"Booyakah, Booyakah!" charged Saba, imitating the moves of the Jamaican dancehall queens. Princess gathered her pajamas and toothbrush laughing all the way into the bathroom. Just as she was about to squeeze the toothpaste out, Stephanie walked in.

"Princess, I'm gonna tell you somethin'. Watch yourself with Sherita. She'll act like your friend, try to get all into your business and then sting you like a snake."

A pang of tension came over Princess as she sensed trouble in the tone of Stephanie's words. "Sherita?"

"Don't sleep on her, I'm telling you. And Terry's like . . . her fantasy."

"I see she's always in his—"

"What! She was trying to throw herself at him before you got here, and he didn't want to have anything to do with her. That's why she's got an attitude. She can't stand the fact that he's talking to you."

"You lyin'!" Princess said, feeling her heart beginning to race.

"Look . . . she was grinnin' up with you when you first came here to keep an eye on things, especially when she found out Terry was sniffin' around."

"But I'm not even going out with him yet."

"Doesn't matter. She wants him whether *you* want him or not. So I'm telling you now—watch yourself."

The squeak of the door signaled someone coming. Two other girls from the floor came in, heading straight for the shower.

"I got to be up early for practice," Stephanie said, quickly changing the subject as she went into one of the bathroom stalls.

Princess brushed her teeth fast and hard, mulling over Stephanie's words. *This isn't my imagination, then. This girl really wants Terry.* After rinsing her mouth, she raised her head and saw Sherita walk in.

Curfew was less than thirty minutes away. Princess lowered her head and doused her face with water. Grabbing the towel, she dried her skin, gently tapping the wet areas. Sherita's icy glare was all over her. She could feel it.

"How you gonna just ignore me like that?" Sherita asked, leaning on the sink, folding her arms squarely in front of her. "And who bought you that rose?"

"I wasn't ignoring you. I didn't mean to tell you," Princess replied coldly.

Sherita drew up a plastic smile. "So what's the big deal?"

"It's a secret," Princess said and headed for the shower. "My secret."

THE DESK Mrs. DeMarco assigned to Princess in the newspaper office was equipped with a laptop and telephone. She was swamped with e-mail and anonymous letters sent in response to her column. Thrilled that her idea was well-received and the responses so numerous, she eagerly read every one of them.

Most of the information was so off the wall, she realized that it could never be published. Some responses were simply frivolous. But other news seemed to serve as a long-awaited outlet for students to vent about themselves, but mostly about others.

One girl claimed to have seen a UFO on campus and that as a result, all students had been transformed. Her submission read like a science fiction story:

> They landed after midnight. At 2:02am on a Tuesday morning a tremendous thunderstorm flooded the earth. The beaming lights of a capsule lit up the grounds and froze the entire campus. The rain came to an abrupt stop and a residue of heavy smoke prevailed. Tiny creatures of varying dimensions appeared out of sliding eye-like doors. One by one they came, searching for human prey. There was no language among them; they communicated by the twitching of their ears. While we were asleep, their bodies penetrated our walls and they inhabited our physical beings. Those creatures have now taken on our appearances and are wandering the earth disguised as us. We must all bond together and find some antidote or miracle that will suffocate these creatures so that we can return to our earthly selves.

Princess couldn't tell if another letter was from a boy or a girl. It read:

> Getting ripped is the sure way to a great SAT score. For all you hard-working students that studied, use the

marijuana prep course next time and be guaranteed a good score. I have the evidence to prove it.

With the clock ticking close to the deadline for the new issue, the writers for the political section were in a hot debate over the war in Iraq and its impact on oil prices. Princess read and absorbed each letter, giving each of them equal consideration. Then she separated the letters into files that she felt had the most promise.

Some read like public service commercials, speaking out against tobacco or encouraging abstinence. 'Burnout' was the subject of one. Its subtitle read: *Hair caught on fire because she tried to light up a cigarette or some weed after 'lights out.'* Princess immediately thought about Saba, but no such thing had happened—not to her knowledge, anyway. Another person wrote a warning that said:

> Beware the popular sport—unprotected sex. STD also stands for Sam Tom and Dave. It's running rampant. Don't get caught with them because you will get smoked.

A pang of shame teased her. What had she started? And it didn't get any better. One letter simply said:

> Some bodies—were caught in the chapel doing the 'nasty.' News at 11:00.

Oh my God! They rollin' like that up here? In the chapel? No way!

Another student wrote mysteriously:

Students are on the edge, and a painless departure could be the answer to quiet all the madness.

Okay, is there a vigilante on campus or is somebody on a suicide mission? Jesus! Goose pimples ran along Princess' arms as she sifted through more disturbing mail.
Uh-oh, here's another one:

Beware. Two white, naked males roaming the campus at night may be armed, potentially dangerous, said to be desperately seeking souls. I can hear their voices.

Finally, Princess came upon a decent story. One girl explained how academic pressure leads to obesity.

If eating yourself into oblivion is what intense studying leads to, then what's the point? In America, fat is not a characteristic of success. It's one or the other.

Oh, I can't wait to tell Nadira this. One e-mail particularly interested Princess:

When girls mature beyond their male contemporaries, what do you do? Soul mating on the Internet is the choice for romance in the twenty-first century. That's what I did. Who says you have to be physically present to get to know someone? The connection is real when you're communicating from the heart. I know all about him. He knows all about me and we've never actually met. But on the next weekend pass, we will. Wish me luck. -ELCEE.

Princess massaged the strain she felt pulling at the back of her neck and paused for a time-out. As a tingly sensation arose, she found her mind wandering. Suddenly, she saw a large crowd of people making a mad dash, running away. There were cars parked in a wide-open space and someone was screaming. Then, the screen of her mind went hazy gray . . . *What was that all about?* Princess wondered with dread.

Shaking off the strange vision, Princess pondered the selections and came up with three categories for the upcoming issue: Romance, Personally Speaking, and Tips to CIO, (Cash in On). For each of them, Princess selected three stories to submit for final approval.

"Good job, Princess," Mrs. DeMarco commended as she whizzed past her. A group of students followed her, scurrying toward her office. The quick smiles and taps on her computer were congratulations, Boravia-style. Princess smiled back, wondering if the student staff had written some of those letters to her. In a sense, she felt privileged that she had opened up a line of communication among students and that they felt free to unload some of their troubles on her. *Not bad for a girl from Telham Park.*

Following the letters, seventeen e-mail messages awaited her attention, including one from Nadira.

From: "Nadira Watford"
To: "Princess Brixton"
Subject: GirlTalk

What's Up Sis?

Reading your messages gave me the chills. O.K., I'm ready to pack my bags and come up there—now! No seriously, the school sounds too good to be true. I'm really considering going to a boarding school, if my parents would let me. I don't care about the hard work, I'm used to that. This guy Terry sounds like potential. Give me the details on the other particulars, know what I'm sayin'. If everything checks out, then I would proceed—with caution.

Christopher asks me about you every day, as if I have you on radar. The girls are like vultures now trying to get him to change course, but he's not having it. His heart is set on the one and only. Harold is still doing his regular, but I don't know. I'm not feeling him like that. Yeah, yeah, I know what you're thinking. I know him well from school and church, he's an athlete and all that but... Maybe he has to grow on me. In the meantime I want to see what the rest of the world has to offer.

This place is just not the same without you. Still a little crazy though. There was a bomb threat like three days in a row at school and we had to evacuate the building. The first time it happened they let us go home. Cops were everywhere. Helicopters flew over the school like it was some terrorist threat. But then other rumors said the Eastern Thugs were trying to get some of those guys they wanted out of the building.

Speaking of the Thugs, remember the day when the cops arrested Jaydee and Tyreek. Well, come to find out they were the ones who bum rushed Jon Lee's Fish Market last week. They tried to rob the old man but he wasn't having it. While they were busy stealing the money Jon Lee caught them off guard with some Kung Fu action. People said fish was flying everywhere. The man fought them so hard they had to get up out of there. But then, Tyreek slipped and fell into a basket of shrimp and that's when Jon Lee caught him, beat him down and pulled off his cap. Once he saw his face, it was over.

Hey, you know Mrs. Rice is winning the Great Trumpet Award for that Black History book she wrote. The school announced it and gave her a plaque at a special assembly. We saw her on the news, too. I've never seen her happier. The ceremony is being held in some big hotel in Manhattan. She invited my parents to come.

The Supreme Steppers are out of control. We got four shows coming back to back, so rehearsals are intense. I still turn my head to your position expecting you to be there when individual drills are called. That's when I feel the void the most. I miss you like crazy. Oh yeah, and before I forget— McCuller's is having a big Masquerade party. You gonna be there, right? All the gang is cool. Everybody sends their love. Mom and Dad send hugs and kisses. Call me after church on Sunday.

LYLAS
(Love Ya Like A Sister)

seven

Princess and Nadira were picnicking on the roof, collecting lottery tickets when they heard an explosion. Looking down, they saw Finley, a neighborhood friend, being handcuffed by policemen on motorcycles. Then her mother called her and they were on a boat, and there was nothing but water as far as she could see. The school cafeteria at Telham Park was closing and she bagged some oatmeal raisin cookies, but then realized her favorite baseball was missing, so she took to the jungle, looking for it.

Opening her eyes from the strange pattern of events she dreamed, Princess stretched her limbs, luxuriating in the rays of the strong Indian summer sun filtering through her window. Grateful that it was Saturday with an opportunity to sleep late, she fell back on to her bed, thinking. Then she got up, took a long, hot, invigorating shower, and the privacy of primping and prancing while listening to soothing music was a welcome reprieve.

By noon, Princess felt energized, optimistic, and adventurous. With mild temperatures and warm winds, it was a perfect day for riding horses and a chance to see Terry. The nearly mile-long hike to the Equestrian Center conjured up memories of her past. The smell of horses and hay took Princess back to Timmonsville, South Carolina, her grandmother's hometown, where she visited every other summer. The farm had been her first taste of true freedom—walking barefoot on lush grass, basking in the sunshine and delighting in super-sweet, organically grown watermelon—on a wide-open field canvassing little girl dreams.

"Princess!" Terry called, spotting her from the outdoor arena, waving madly to get her attention. He hurried toward her with brisk strides as if she were a mirage that might disappear.

She hardly recognized him with his cowboy hat on, which made him look ruggedly handsome. "Aaay! Look at you."

"What's goin' on, little girl?"

"Nothin' much. Thought I'd come up here and check it out."

"This is another side of my world," he said glaring, an ear-to-ear smile spread across his face. "You like it?"

Princess' eyes scanned the 13-acre facility and returned back to him, noticing the diamond stud earring in his right ear. "From what I can see . . . yeah."

"Come over here," Terry directed, grabbing her hand and leading her into the training arena. "Let me introduce you to somebody," he said, heading toward the unattended Arabian stallion. With twenty feet between them, Princess stopped abruptly, forcefully squeezing Terry's hand.

"What's the matter?"

"I don't know about him."

"Him? You mean the horse?"

Princess didn't respond. She simply stared at the massiveness of the animal.

"Aw, you scared," Terry realized, laughing. "Nothing to be scared about. We call her Satin."

Princess looked incredulously at Terry, wondering what part of this he didn't understand.

"It's a she," he added easily, as if the fact that the horse was female would assuage Princess' fears. "She's harmless, let me show you." He gently inched her closer, inventing conversation to try to distract her fear.

When Satin turned her proud head and flowing mane and blinked her prominent eyes, Princess stopped cold and snatched her hand out of Terry's grip. "He's looking at me!"

"No, *she's* looking at you. Just trying to be friendly, that's all. Come on."

Princess shook her head defiantly, backing away from Terry. She was so scared she could hardly feel her feet against the pea gravel.

"There's nothing to be afraid of," he said, drawing Princess closer.

But fear continued to stiffen her mobility.

"Come on, girl." Terry embraced her and drew her toward him. She resisted even more. Putting some force on his pull, he was able to get her feet moving. But then, consumed by fear, Princess bent her knees and squatted, planting her footing in the gravel. "Nnn . . . no, I can't do this."

"I gotchu," Terry assured, forcefully easing her up on her feet. "You know I wouldn't let anything happen to you."

"No, I know, but . . . I don't see it."

"It's all in your mind. Look, I'll be riding Satin. You're just holding on to me. Think about it like that."

Holding on tight to Terry, she took a deep breath and decided to trust him. "Okay . . . but don't move too fast."

"Alright. Come on, loosen up . . . shake off that fear," he encouraged, taking short steps. "If Satin thinks you're scared, she's going to be scared, too. Inch up a little closer, we're almost there."

Gingerly, Terry began stroking the top of Satin's head and on down her back. "See, you gotta stroke her real gentle-like. Then she'll become familiar with your touch. But it can't be a scared touch . . . 'cause she won't trust you. C'mon, let's walk her first." He grabbed Satin's reins and wrapped them around his hand and slapped her side.

"Where we goin'?" Princess asked.

"For a little walk around the stable . . . get to know her." Locking arms with Princess, they began a leisurely stroll. "Horses are one of the easiest animals to train, believe it or not. It's all in the way you handle them. My uncle showed me that from way back. I used to ride all over the place with him at home. Then he went on the road with the Black Rodeo."

"Black Rodeo?"

"Yeah . . . you never heard of it?"

"Nope."

"They're all over the country now."

"So you've been in rodeo shows before?"

"Nah, 'cause by the time they hit the road I was already in school—like what . . . second grade. But whenever my uncle was around, he would take me riding. I was scared like you at first, wouldn't go near 'em. But one day, he straddled me up there, jumped on behind me and took off. There wasn't a feeling in the world like it, and I've been riding ever since."

"Wow."

Out of the gate of the indoor arena galloped a chestnut-colored American Warmblood, a powerful horse with strong, elastic gaits. "There's Mr. Conway, the instructor. He's gotta spot-check us when we're riding. That's the rules if I'm taking out a beginner."

"So who do you ride with out here?"

"I'm usually by myself. Once in a while my boys come out, but they're not really into it like that."

Princess eyeballed Mr. Conway's horsemanship, communicating direction without saying a word.

"Did you eat yet?" Terry turned and asked.

"No."

"Good. I meant to tell you not to. People sometime get sick to their stomach when they ride a horse for the first time. Not used to the motion."

"Uh oh."

"Nah, you'll be alright," Terry said, pulling her close to him.

"Picked a good day for riding," said the instructor galloping toward them. He was a youngish, well-built white man with bushy brown hair, a thick mustache, and gray eyes.

"Mr. Conway, this is Princess."

"Hello, Princess. Welcome."

"Hello, Mr. Conway."

He doffed his hat to them and asked, "Ready to go?"

"In a minute," Terry told him.

Mr. Conway then swung his horse around and took off, kicking up a lot of dust.

"He looks like he's enjoying himself," said Princess.

"Oh, yeah. Mr. Conway would ride up and down all of Pennsylvania if he could. Now you got the ultimate protection, me and him, so let's get up on Satin. We just gonna give this big girl a little exercise."

Princess swallowed hard, tensely alert, and braced herself—for anything.

"Now put your right foot in the stirrup right here, and swing your other leg around her."

"What if he takes off?"

Terry laughed ardently. "No Princess, *she* doesn't do anything she's not instructed to do. You know, like how women s'posed to behave."

"You think that's funny?"

"A little light humor never hurt a scared first-timer. Come on."

"Wait!"

"For what? Satin's ready."

"Okay . . . just don't let me go."

"I won't . . . I promise."

Princess lifted herself up with Terry's help. She held on to his arm so tightly she could feel her fingers sinking into his skin. "Carry your leg over, and just ease into the saddle."

Terry jumped on Satin behind Princess, and his weight caused the horse to move. A heavy gasp came out of her as he skillfully controlled the reins. "You okay?"

"I think so."

"Just hold on," Terry said. "We're ready to move. When Mr. Conway comes, he'll ride close to us."

Princess looked at the other students riding freely, trying to distract her fear. "Those are the pros I see."

"Oh, yeah," Terry acknowledged, pulling the reins as they trotted off. Once Princess relaxed, Satin's movements felt as natural as walking.

"Feeling better now?"

"Uh huh."

"You remind me of my little sister," he said, chuckling. "She won't go near a horse without me. Be 'bout ta squeeze me to death."

"Aww, you gotta little sister?"

"Yeah, that's my heart. She's only ten."

"I always wanted a sister—and a brother."

"You're an only child?"

"It's just me."

"So I bet you were scared to come to this school, right?"

"Not really scared, I just didn't want to come. I heard all these great things about this place, but leaving home . . . my friends and everything . . . to live in some historic museum with all these strangers. I didn't know if I could deal with it, but . . . look at what's up here compared to what we have back at home."

"No comparison. It's a different world—their world. I shouldn't say that 'cause there's a couple of brothers up here from families that got loot, too. Blair's pop owns a chain of restaurants. David and Robert, I don't think you know them; they're graduating this year. Both of them come from families with deep pockets. They're into real estate."

"Did you want to come here?" Princess asked.

"For the scholarship? Heck, yeah. I was all wit' it. I didn't want to leave my family and all that, specially my mom . . . but I was looking at the bigger picture. This might be their world, but me coming here is gonna prepare me to make my own world."

"I feel you. So, you came here on the basketball scholarship?"

"Yeah, but my grades were pretty good, too. And I scored big-time on the entrance exam, so I would've got in either way."

Terry pulled the reins and they began to pick up the pace. Riding Satin felt like dancing at high speed high off the ground.

"See, it's all in the personality. I like a cool, even tempered, kick-but horse . . . one that you never see coming.

Some of 'em are just bold and powerful. That's cool too, if that's what you like. But I prefer a level-headed horse that I can control."

"What makes a horse lose control and throw people off?"

"When something scares 'em, like a bolt of lightening, a firecracker, or a gunshot, they go crazy. They'll throw you off in a minute. Or . . . if they experienced something bad when they were young, they never forget it. My uncle told me horses have a long memory for things that scare them, like barking dogs and wild animals, stuff like that. That'll make them jump and run, too."

Terry pulled the reins, gave Satin a hard smack with a riding crop, and she raced off. Princess held tightly to his arms, closed her eyes, and prayed.

"See, it's a smooth ride," he said, pressing his face on the side of hers. Satin's an American Quarter, the kind of horse that cops ride. "You're in good hands and Conway is right behind us. C'mon, Satin!"

They rode throughout the back boundary of the campus along the horse trail for what seemed like forever. Princess had no idea the land extended out so far. Terry slowed Satin down when they passed a wide, three-story building made of light crème-colored brick, with big bay windows and forest-green awnings.

"Look at that," Princess said, admiring the botanical garden of plants displayed through the clear glass of the third level conservatory.

"That's the horticulture building," Terry told her.

Close by was a lake where students were socializing, eating at picnic tables, lounging on the grass with their laptops and some were simply relaxing and soaking up the sun. All of the tragic thoughts about what might happen while she was riding had disappeared.

"I see you smiling now, uh oh," Terry teased as they trotted back to the stable. "Riding opens you up. Gets your mind to workin'."

"Sure does."

"Think you can ride by yourself?"

"Okay, now you're pushin' it. Hey, do your parents ride?"

"Nah. My mother's got high blood pressure. She can hardly stand to watch *me* on the trail. Couldn't picture her ridin'."

"What about your father?"

"What about him?" Terry responded dryly.

"Oooh, that's not a good sound." She allowed the silence to drift between them, figuring he would answer when he felt ready.

"When my mom and dad split up, so did we. I mean, I see him sometimes. We talk a little bit . . . tries to act like he's the great father and all that—"

"Heard it before, only I don't remember my parents ever being together. They split up before I was born."

"I'd never leave my kids, I'll tell you that right now."

"I don't see it, either."

"Especially if I was making little princes and princesses with you."

An elbow to the stomach caught him by surprise. "What did I say?"

The stable had become livelier now, as more students had come out to ride. "Ooooh, look at them," Princess said pointing to the group of students wearing formal riding attire: the jacket, helmet, pants, and boots. "Oh, that's hot! Are they a team or something?"

"Nah, just the rich kids who like to ride in full gear."

I would love to wear some riding gear like that. Take pictures and send them to my friends back at home. They wouldn't believe it.

Dismounting Satin wasn't nearly as difficult for Princess as getting on had been.

"Wasn't so bad now, was it?" Terry asked, trotting toward the steel horse stables.

"Not at all." Princess smiled, sincerely appreciative of the experience.

"Here we go, Satin," said Terry, leading her into the stall. "You're back home." Terry began brushing Satin to cool her down. "Ready to eat?" he asked.

"You feed her?"

"Sometimes," he replied, matting, picking and tidying up the area. "They've got staff to do the feedin' and the breedin.' " Intrigued, Princess shadowed Terry, observing the process of equine maintenance. He then removed his saddle and stored it in the equipment area, which was in the next stall. Bales of hay were stacked up along the wall in one section. Feed, pitchforks, and grooming aids were in another.

Princess helped, feeding Satin orchard grass and alfalfa. Now unafraid, Princess rubbed Satin's head as they were about to leave. "Be good now."

"Still ridin', huh?" Terry asked, exiting the stall.

"What?"

"I bet you feel like you're still riding."

Princess chuckled at the truth of his words. She could still feel the rolling rhythm in her rear and legs. "How did you know that?"

" 'Cause I know these things. You alright?"

"I'm good," she replied, admiring the riders on horseback galloping past them, already imagining herself doing the same thing one day. "Hmm, none of those horses look like Satin," Princess noticed. "They're all different . . . like people, with their own personalities."

"There you go. You're feeling 'em now. And the more you ride 'em, the more they begin to feel like people. They got moods and attitudes, but they're big and strong, so you got to know how to control them. When you can do that . . . they'll take you anywhere you want to go."

"You like being in control, huh?"

"Well, if the opposite of control is chaos, I want to be in control."

"Sounds like you used to be out of control."

Terry chuckled, bobbing his head up and down. "You're good boy," he said, referring to himself. "Can spot 'em a million miles away."

"What are you talkin' about?" Princess looked puzzled.

"When somebody can *feel* you, that's like hittin' the jackpot. See how you knew that about me?"

"Wasn't hard to figure out."

"Yo, I used to be a terror. Mad at the world. I would get into trouble at school and they would call my mom. When I get home she would tear my butt up and I'd be right back at it again the next day."

"I can see that in you."

"That's what I'm talking about. I know how to find a girl that's got some eyes and ears. Females don't usually listen to me when I talk . . . or feel me."

"Why not?"

"I don't know. They're usually somewhere else. You want to get something to eat?"

"In a few."

Switching course from the clubhouse, they walked along the observation deck of the indoor training pen.

"Ohmigosh! Look at that," Princess quivered. Inside the fenced yard was a cream-colored horse with a white mane and tail running wildly.

"That's Ginger," said Terry. "All fifteen-hundred pounds of her."

"What's she doing?" asked Princess, admiring the draft breed's amber eyes.

"Just playing around. It's good to let them run free sometimes. That's how you develop their trust."

They stopped and watched the instructor tame the American Cream with simple gestures made with his elbows and by the easy wave of his arms like he was performing magic.

"Horses are something else," Princess said, following Ginger's graceful movements. The horse trainer slowed her down nice and easy. Gradually, Ginger came to a complete standstill.

"Check this out," Terry said excitedly.

The horse folded her legs underneath and allowed her body to fall to the ground.

"Oh, snap! How did he do that?" Princess bellowed, awe-struck. She had never witnessed anything like that before; never even knew it was possible.

"It's all in the training. Not easy though, 'cause getting that horse to lie down is like . . . the hardest thing to do."

Princess watched the horse as long as she could as they began to walk.

"Uh oh, don't tell me my girl is gettin' hooked on horses."

"They're interesting."

"Yeah, they can be . . . like I'm interested in you."

He slipped his hand inside hers as the heat of the early afternoon sun intensified. They stopped near the home of the headmaster, Mr. Delmore. It was a three-story brick Georgian-style home sitting on a hill that overlooked the campus. A picturesque water fountain, spewing water in criss-cross directions and flowing down into a little pond highlighted the landscaping in front, so lush and verdant.

"My house is gonna be bigger than that. Ever seen Barbo's house, the boxer?"

"No."

"Fifty-seven thousand square feet, yo, on something like . . . forty acres."

"That's enough land to have your own stable," Princess said.

"Huh, two or three."

A cool breeze swept across their faces and a blanket of crunchy leaves shuffled underfoot as they slowed to a stroll by the lake. Noticeable numbers of students were out there now, including a group of white girls who stared at them as they passed.

"Your fans are watching you."

"No, not my type."

"You mean you wouldn't hook up with one of them?"

"Why should I when the honey here is *overflowing*."

Princess thought about Snoopy. "No, seriously. You wouldn't hook up with a white girl?"

"I look like I got the fever?"

"You sayin' something's wrong with it?"

"Nah, I'm just sayin' to each man his pleasure, but it's not my *flava*. Plus, I ain't tryin' to put myself out there like that 'cause somebody wants to sample the goods, know what I'm sayin'?"

"What if it's the real thing . . . coming from the heart?"

"That's cool. But my moms, she wouldn't have it. You think *their parents* don't like it? My moms and grandma, shoot . . . they would come at me with some blows from the ancestors."

"Whether people like it or not, a whole lot of it's goin' on around here."

"Whatchu know about that?"

" 'Small Talk,' remember?"

"Okay," Terry smiled, lowering his eyes. "So you probably already know a little bit about everything going on around here."

"Not everything, but I hear a lot."

Halfway around the lake, they stopped and looked out onto the still water.

Terry threw an imaginary ball through an imaginary hoop."This is the place where I like to dream."

"Dream about what?"

"Life. The NBA. My own legal practice. A big house with a tennis court, a horse stable . . . and a Princess."

"Yeah, okay. So you really want to study law?"

"Yep." Terry threw another imaginary ball.

"So, you got a brain up there, too?"

He did a double take while Princess pretended not to see him. "There's a whole lot a brain in there," he said and threw another ball.

"So, you want to practice law after the NBA? Like entertainment law?"

"Nah, nah, criminal."

"Whoa, I feel you. Whole lot of brothers out there doin' time . . . innocent ones, too."

"That's what I like about you, you got ears, girl. Kinda mature to be fifteen."

"I'll be sixteen on my birthday."

"No! A whole sixteen," he mimicked, holding his hand to his chest like a girl. "Oh, my God!"

"Stop playin'," Princess said, shoving him.

"Oooh . . . you're strong too. Different, alright."

"Guess so. At home they call me the 'old spirit.' "

"Oh, you mean like you been here before?"

"Something like that."

"Okay then, let's sit at that bench over there. Then you can tell me all about your former life."

Princess faced the water while Terry sat sideways and faced her.

"Ummm, that's a pretty sight," he commented, gazing at Princess with the sky as her background.

"Beautiful," Princess added, following the lake's continuous ripples.

"I'm not talking about the water."

Princess shot Terry a quick glance and moved away.

"Don't be shy, come back to me," he said, sliding his arm around her shoulders and pulling her toward him.

"I don't consider myself shy."

"Okay, maybe not shy . . . just something about the way you—"

"Cautious, a little. Best way to be."

"So you gonna be my girl at the Social?"

Princess looked at him blankly, unimpressed with his offer, but moreso in the way he asked.

"Alright, let me come again with that." He sighed, straightened himself up and then turned on an authentic-sounding British accent. "Would you please do me the honor of allowing me to escort you to the Millennium Social, your Royal Highness?"

Princess couldn't contain her laughter and now knew he was serious. "Let me think about it."

"Alright."

"Since when do you wear an earring?" Princess asked, shifting the attention away from her.

"This was my mom's earring. She lost the other one so she gave it to me." Terry gently rubbed the diamond stud. "I forgot I had it on. Hardly ever wear it 'cept when I ride. Keeps me safe."

Terry removed the earring from his ear. "And if you wear it, my protection will be multiplied . . . maybe my luck, too." His firm hands patiently removed Princess' earring from her right ear and gently inserted his.

"What are you gonna do with mine?"

"Give it back to you. Here. Just wear mine . . . okay?"

"Okay."

Terry tipped his hat backward, reached over and kissed Princess on the nape of her neck, his warm breath caressing her skin. "Can't you see us together?"

"Umm huh," she replied, sliding her tongue over her lips, anticipating a kiss.

Terry turned her face slowly toward his. When he pressed his soft lips against hers, the world melted into one great big ball of perfection. Princess backed away for a moment, peering into the translucent depth of his inviting eyes. He kissed her again. Telham Park, her family, friends and all of the circles of her existence moved further away from her mind. He kissed her again, and time seemed to stop. No recall of problems or worries or thoughts of tomorrow. There was only this beautiful day, this wonderful time, this perfect moment.

eight

L ate autumn days turned crisp and chilly, the kind that inspired teen love affairs and long-cherished personal memories. As the daylight hours diminished, Princess and Terry tried to spend more time together. Stealing brief moments between their busy schedules—a lunch here, dinner there, Saturday and Sunday afternoon horseback riding or stealing kisses by the lake—made it all the more thrilling.

Princess was also gathering pleasant memories at Boravia among the girls in her suite, who were growing on her like family—at least all but one. They shared clothes just as easily as they shared books, music and ideas. Saba even asked Princess to cornrow her hair one evening, showing her appreciation of African braids and other multicultural nuances. This led other white girls on the campus to have their hair cornrowed. However, Sherita remained noticeably distant with Princess—she was often absent from activities, subdued and said very little.

By nine that Sunday evening Princess was exhausted. Earlier, following morning chapel, Ms. Morgan had treated a group of them to a brunch at Ridgeland's International House of Pancakes, where they feasted on a buffet of breakfast favorites, dinner treats and seafood delicacies.

R&B music played softly as everyone prepared for bed. A sharp, pecking sound piqued the interest of those who heard it, but no one said anything at first.

"Did you hear that, Saba?" Princess asked when she heard it again.

"I sure did. I thought I was losin' it 'cause I heard it a few times."

"What's the matter? Snoopy asked.

"Shhhhhh! Turn off your music," Princess directed Saba.

Tyler's head bobbled to the music coming from her iPod while she painted her toenails fiery red. Saba flew over to her and snatched her earphones off of her ears.

"What are you doing?"

"Sounds like something's in here. It's a strange noise."

"You been smokin' weed again?"

"I'm not paranoid," she replied, silencing her music and the strange pecking sounded again.

"There it is, you heard it?"

Tyler immediately put the nailbrush back into the bottle and stood up, listening.

Sherita snatched the hot curlers out of her hair and leaped onto her bed. "I hope we don't have any little friends running around here," she said, referring to mice.

"Making noise like that, are you kidding?" Saba's eyes grew large in curiosity as she moved to the center of the room. For a split second there was absolute silence and all they could hear was the water beating against the tiles in the shower.

Sherita held onto her hairbrush as if it were a weapon, ready to strike at any moment.

"And what are ya supposed to be doing with that?" Snoopy asked.

Again, the noise sounded from the corner of the room near Saba's bed. At once they all jumped, really scared this time. Sherita and Snoopy headed for the door.

"Wait!" Tyler urged. "It came from the window."

"It sure did," Princess agreed. She and Tyler tiptoed over to the window, facing the east side of the campus. At night there was little to be seen between the giant trees except the winding road that led to the reservoir.

"Call Ms. Morgan," Snoopy said.

"Shhhhhh!" Tyler signaled. "Don't do that yet. Wait. You see anything, Princess?"

"No."

Saba inched between them and pressed her face to the window, looking down. "Somebody's out there. Look!"

". . . It's Stephanie!" Tyler realized.

"What the heck is she doing out there?" asked Saba.

"I haven't the slightest." As Tyler struggled to get the window opened wider, a sweep of cold air rushed in, causing the girls to shiver. She stuck her head out and waved. Making a silent gesture, Stephanie pointed her thumbs upward and used the sturdy ceramic grill on the buildings' exterior—a restoration highlight—as her foot ladder to get to the second floor.

"I don't believe it," said Tyler. "She's climbing up."

"Oh, she's lost it now," Saba declared.

"Don't let her do that!" Snoopy screeched, horrified.

"Shhhhhh!" Tyler urged, monitoring Stephanie's movement. With the technique and efficiency of an accomplished mountain climber, Stephanie moved on up with natural dexterity.

"My God!" Snoopy shrieked, terrified. "If she falls we'll be in some kind of trouble."

"We?" asked Sherita. "Uh uh, not me."

"Stop her!" wailed Snoopy.

"No!" Tyler persisted, confident in Stephanie's athletic ability. "Don't distract her. She'll make it."

"I don't understand," said Snoopy. "She doesn't have climbing equipment so how is she—"

Unexpectedly, the door flew open and Tiara burst in. "What's going on?" Everybody gasped in surprise.

Saba thought fast, moving toward her. "We're having a pajama jammy," she explained hastily, shoving Tiara out the door. "And you're not invited!"

"Lights out in a minute," Tiara reminded them from the other side of the door.

"That scared me to death," Snoopy said, pressing her hand against her thumping heart.

"Keep your eyes on that door," Saba commanded flying back to the window.

Tyler, Saba and Princess reached out of the window to yank Stephanie inside. Ignoring their questions, Stephanie immediately began peeling off her clothes. It was nine-twenty six p.m.

"When Ms. Morgan comes in I've been here since seven," Stephanie instructed, breathing heavily, "but I was down in study hall and when I came in I jumped in the shower and went to sleep." Down to her underwear, she shoved her street clothes under the bed. "Tyler, hand me a shirt."

"*But where have you been?*" Princess asked.

"And why did you come in through the window?" grilled Snoopy.

Stephanie put on the shirt and pulled the covers over her head, dismissing all of their questions. "We'll talk later."

Ms. Morgan was admonishing someone, and upon hearing her voice the girls turned off the lights and scattered to their beds like scared rabbits. "Suite 210 girls, it's time." The door opened, catching everyone settling under the covers. "Tyler, have you heard from Stephanie this evening?"

". . . Sure I have. She's right here."

Ms. Morgan turned on the lights and walked over to her bed. "Stephanie. Stephanie."

"Yes," she answered in a sleepy voice.

"Where have you been?"

"Huh?" she replied, looking around feigning grogginess.

"You didn't return your weekend pass. I didn't think you were here and I was just about to call your parents."

"Umm, no need for that," she yawned. "They dropped me off earlier this evening and I went to study hall."

"And why didn't you bring me your pass? You know the rules."

"I'd been there so long . . . I guess I forgot. Then I came up here and took a shower." She gave off a long yawn, stretched and fell back sleepily onto her pillow. "I gotta be up at six for practice and I'm kinda tired."

"Alright, Stephanie, but your weekend pass is critical. It must be in my hand no later than 7:30 on Sunday."

"Okay."

"Sorry to disturb you, ladies," she whispered, turning off the lights. "Have a good night."

"Goodnight, Ms. Morgan," they replied in concert.

Covers turned back. Stephanie raised up and everyone, except Sherita, raced over to her.

"I freaked when I saw you outside the window," Saba sharply uttered. "What are you doing? You know its past curfew."

"Where have you been?" charged Princess.

"Wait a minute. Let me—"

"Bloody oh, what were ya thinkin'?" asked Tyler.

"I've seen some drama, but this is *extra*," mumbled Sherita from her bed.

"What was that?" asked Stephanie.

"You heard me."

Snoopy shoved her "You know what kind of trouble we would have been in. If these walls could talk they would be telling everybody how—"

Just then the door flew open and Ms. Morgan peered in. "Girls, special assembly tomorrow at three. There's gonna be a guest appearance by Congressman Delano, so remain in uniform after class. Time for bed. Now!"

The door echoed after it slammed. Snoopy's eyes were shut tight. Princess went numb. Stephanie trembled inside.

"I've got a bit of a knot in my stomach," Tyler said quietly.

"I need a cigarette," Saba muttered.

"You think she noticed anything?" asked Snoopy.

The thought was too chilling for anyone to entertain. One by one they retreated to their beds in the darkness, and for a few moments everyone was quiet.

"Where were you?" Snoopy questioned Stephanie.

"Yeah, and why did you climb up here? What if you would have fallen? I was scared to death," whispered Princess.

"I was trying to get your attention," Stephanie explained. "I couldn't yell out loud; other people would have heard me. So I started throwing rocks at the window."

"Then why didn't you just come through the front door?" Snoopy pried.

"It was locked!"

"But you could have—"

"Why didn't you call from the security gate?" Saba probed.

"Shhh!" Stephanie warned. "I couldn't call from there 'cause my parents brought me through the gate since from like six o' clock and I signed in. Since I was early, I went to the Armory to watch Damien practice."

"Again, Stephanie! I knew it," Saba remarked in a judgmental puff. "Practice didn't last all night, so where were you?"

"I went to Damien's room. Nobody was around so I snuck in and he had his friend bring us some pizza."

"You did what!" exclaimed Sherita.

"It took you that long to eat a pizza?" Tyler questioned.

"Well, we needed some personal time and . . . we just lost track."

"He's got his own room, right?" Princess asked.

"Yeah, and?"

"Are you kidding? What if someone had seen you in there? 'Cause that's not the place to get caught in. I'd be receiving mad e-mails for 'Small Talk' in the morning about you."

"I hope you put in a side order of a little sumthin' sumthin' from the pharmacy to go along with that pizza," Sherita quibbled sarcastically.

"What's Health-Aid got to do with pizza?" Snoopy asked.

"Oh God, tell me she just didn't ask me that," Sherita muttered. Pillows and teddy bears flew from all corners of the room at Snoopy.

"After it got so late, I ran here and the door was already locked," Stephanie continued. "I couldn't go to security. Couldn't call anybody, so I did what I had to do."

"Oh, so you climb up two stories. Are you loony?" asked Saba. "You could've killed yourself."

"Nah, that was—"

"Meanwhile, you could've given any one of us a heart attack," Princess said.

"My heart is still racing," Saba exclaimed and hopped out of bed, reaching for a cigarette under the mattress. "I need a smoke."

"Not in here, you're not," Stephanie insisted.

"You shut up! If we can pull you out of a window to save your butt, then I can have a smoke."

"No, Saba, we'll get in trouble," Snoopy pleaded.

"This place makes me crazy! Alright, get a grip. I'll go to the bathroom."

"Good!" everybody agreed.

Feeling her way to the door, Saba changed her mind and got back into bed. "Forget it. I'll survive."

A popular rock ringtone startled everybody.

"What's that?" Princess asked.

"Saba's cell," answered Snoopy.

Stephanie fell back onto her pillow, leaving everyone full of anxiety. Saba spoke quietly on the phone underneath the covers even though you could hear what she was saying.

"I'm still shaking," said Tyler. "Do you believe this?"

"I've got to say my prayers," said Snoopy. "And a special one for you, Stephanie."

"Amen to that," Princess agreed.

Eventually they all settled down and surrendered to the late hour, listening to smooth R&B and drifted off to sleep.

nine

'Small Talk' was a magnet to inquiring minds, a welcomed diversion to gossiping gurus, deeming the debut column a huge success. Princess exploded into popularity as students approached her privately, offering tidbits of news. Even Boravia's snobby cliques took notice of her. It had been rumored that Princess might be considered for membership in the Diamond Club, an elite social group of intellectual, accomplished girls. Last year, they had toured the White House as guests of the First Lady, and this year there was talk that it might be Buckingham Palace in London.

At her desk in the newspaper office on Tuesday afternoon, five anonymous letters along with a dozen or so e-mails awaited Princess. The news coming around this time was sizzling hot. A family inheritance just made one of the students a multimillionaire. She wanted to leave school and travel the world. After all, she could afford to.

One girl admitted:

> I'm in love with a man … and he's my teacher. Anonymous.

Another girl updated Princess on her Internet romance, saying:

> I'm convinced. This is really my soul mate and I can't wait to meet him. Traditional courtship is out! Search the soul in him first … then meet him. -ELCEE.

The light tingling creeped at the back of her neck again. In an instant, she visualized a violent struggle between a man and a woman. A panoramic view zoomed in to a line of parked cars. People scattered in a nervous panic. She could see this event despite the fact that her eyes were wide open. Just as suddenly as the vision appeared, her mind returned to a hazy grayness. *I must be pushing myself too hard. Maybe I need to get more sleep.*

Proceeding with her work, she continued to read on. Another note read:

> My best friend's boyfriend is cheating on her—with me! How can I tell her? Signed, Between You and I.

One girl wanted to announce her engagement at the Millennium Social. *This is beginning to sound like a daytime talk show drama and I'm the host.*

"YOU'VE GOT a load of mail today," reported Mrs. Hinckly, the front desk attendant at Bryant Hall.

"For me?" Princess halted. She was making a brief pit stop to change into her street clothes after school.

"Yes, I've got several letters here," she said, shuffling through the last pile of mail. "Ah . . . another one. Here you go."

Receiving four letters in one day was the record so far. Anxious, Princess began opening them and reading as she walked.

Walking down the second-floor corridor, Snoopy backed into Princess accidentally, yelling, "Sherita! Corvette's on the phone."

"Watch it, big girl. Where you goin'?"

"Sorry, Prince, I'm calling in our takeout order. We're getting pizza."

"It's Wednesday already. I forgot!"

"That's right. What do you want?"

"Extra cheese and sausage, and anything to drink."

"You got it."

Princess' mother had written her a note and enclosed a fifty-dollar check that she could deposit in the school bank. Her words were short, to the point, and always ended with the same post-script: "Call me."

Princess then became so engrossed in Christopher's letter, which was three pages long, she almost missed the twenty-dollar bill that was attached to the back of the last page. Nostalgia needled at her in its sneaky, unrelenting way. When Princess wasn't consumed with everything that was happening at school, she missed being home. She wondered what was going on in Telham Park this Wednesday evening.

Tiara and Tyler came into the room babbling non-stop, disturbing Princess' thoughts.

"Show some respect, please."

"Sorry," Tyler apologized. "Was this guy someone she knew?" she asked, lowering her voice.

"Obviously not. She couldn't identify him," Tiara replied.

They walked over to Tyler's bed area, stepping over Stephanie, who was in a full-split position, doing leg stretches. Princess could hear every word they were saying, even though they were trying to be quiet.

"So it definitely wasn't a guy from school?" Tyler probed, sitting on her bed. "Or was it?"

Reading the seriousness of their faces, Saba interjected, "What's going on?"

"It's all over the school," Tyler ushered in. "One of the girls went out on a weekend pass and she was attacked!"

Princess sat up at attention, her ears on full alert.

"By who?" asked Saba.

"Nobody knows," Tiara shrugged.

"Oh my God, was she raped?" Saba's face was turning red.

Tiara shook her head with a spooked look about her. "They're not saying."

"Do we know her?" Princess asked. "What's her name?"

Snoopy entered the room. "Order confirmed. One large, half-sausage, half-pepperoni, the other with extra cheese and a large orange—"

"Lisa Capote," Tyler replied in unintentional disregard. "She's a junior. Lives on the first floor in Nutley Hall."

"Was she out there alone?" Saba asked.

Curious, Snoopy jumped in. "What's going on?"

"One of the upper-class girls was attacked in the mall on a weekend pass," Stephanie explained.

"Oh, no!" Snoopy cried, holding her head between her hands.

"She was with some friends from what I understand," said Tyler. "But she was alone when it happened."

"Where is she now?" Princess asked Tyler.

"Home. The school notified her parents when the police picked her up, but . . . that was on Saturday."

"Saturday?" chorused the group.

"And why are we just hearing about it now?" Snoopy questioned.

"Because the school tried to keep it hush-hush like they always do when something happens," Tiara said, dragging her mysterious gaze from one girl to the other.

"I found out from my friends I eat lunch with," Tyler clarified. "I wasn't there Monday and Tuesday, so I'm just hearing about it today."

"So was the guy stalking her or what?" Saba looked confused.

"Where's this girl from, anyway?" Stephanie's question piggybacked Saba's.

"Somewhere in Boston," answered Tiara.

"Whoa! Her parents must be horrified," remarked Stephanie.

"But why attack her in the mall?" Tyler asked. "I mean her friends said she went to the bathroom and when she stayed away so long, they went looking for her. Security discovered her in the parking lot. Said she had been beaten and was terrified."

"How did she end up in the parking lot from the bathroom?" Princess asked.

"And nobody saw her?" rejoined Snoopy.

"Maybe there's more to this than they're telling us," Tiara surmised. "It has to be."

"Yeah, what if this is just a story," Snoopy commented. "She might be pregnant or something and her boyfriend put out a hit on her because she wants to have the baby and he doesn't, and he comes from this rich family and they don't want their first heir to be from some—"

"Here we go with Sherlock again," Stephanie interrupted. "C'mon, kill it!"

"I don't know," Tiara shrugged. "I don't have a clue."

"There's more to this," Snoopy persisted. "But I know one thing. When we go out together on a weekend pass we're gonna be the Velcro sisters—sticking together like glue."

"That's not gonna be 'til junior year," Saba reminded her.

"It's never too early to start planning."

Princess retreated into her thoughts as she changed into her street clothes. Violence was everywhere, just like her grandmother told her. With all the money and privilege that certain people at Boravia enjoyed, no one was exempt.

From: "Princess Brixton"
To: "Nadira Watford"
Subject: Boravia Update

Nadira,

Sorry I couldn't get back to you before now. I had so much work to do. And there's never enough time in the day. Terry's got me riding on a cloud and during weekends we're riding horses. Yes, and I'm getting hooked on them . . . Terry, too. I'll be his partner at the big party they call the Millennium Social. Auntie is shopping for my dress and shoes right now, and they've got to make a statement, feel me? Now this Sherita is becoming a problem. It's like she's stalking us. Do you think I should confront her?

Oh and listen to this. This white girl from Boston was attacked when she went out on a weekend pass. This so-called great school's got some serious drama going on. Some of the e-mails I receive . . . blow me away! You got some of these girls who are into witchery and Satanism and got that gothic thing going on, where they wear all this black and dark make-up? Then there's a group I call "the slim crew." They're toothpick-thin because they believe that makes them beautiful (bulimia-bound in my opinion). The Republican boys worship money, and one was ready to end his life finding out his stocks have taken a hit. It's all they strategize about, making their investments grow, but on that tip we need to take note, when the economy's pumping again.

Oh, and one of my suitemates almost gave me a heart attack climbing through the window after curfew. Can you believe she was with her boyfriend doing what lovers do after hours, in his room? I had to grab my asthma pump, especially when the housemother came in the room to check. Some of these other girls are messing around with their friends' boyfriends—I mean straight up "doin' 'em."

I heard from Christopher and he asked me to go to the Masquerade party at McCuller's. I don't know—next to Terry, Christopher's shrinking smaller and smaller. If things get really serious with us, I'll have to let him know.

I'm going to send Ms. Rice a congrats card for her book. I'll hit you back when I get a chance.

LYLAS

THE STUDY session for geometry at Morlan Hall lasted longer than Princess had expected. Darkness had descended upon the campus and she appreciated the privacy of the evening walk. She resisted the temptation to stop at the library and steal a kiss from Terry like she did the other night. All studying had ceased after that and they ended up behind the stacks, where things started to heat up.

By the time she reached Bryant Hall, the front door was locked and Mrs. Hinckly had temporarily walked away from the lobby desk.

"Shoot!" Princess banged incessantly on the door, but nobody answered. She stood in the cold air for a full five minutes, which felt more like thirty. Still no one came. Impatiently, Princess proceeded around to the back door and she could hear faint voices volleying back and forth.

"It's like I told you before," a familiar voice pleaded. It was a female.

"Look, nothing's changed, Sherita."

Princess stopped abruptly before cornering the building recognizing Terry's voice.

"Why do you have to talk to me like that?" murmured Sherita, sounding weak and whiny.

"You don't understand English, so I don't have a choice."

"I'm here with you. Doesn't that tell you something?"

"Yo . . . whatever it's saying, Sherita, I'm not tryin' to hear it."

Princess gasped quietly in disbelief; her heart pounded in nervous palpitations. *This can't be happening. Oh my God! Terry and Sherita? Of all the people and places on this campus, how could I would walk in on the two people that—*"

"If you think you're gonna take me there again, yo . . . you don't know."

Oh, so they do know each other, no question about that now. Are they playing me and I'm the last one to know? How could I have been so stupid? There was something behind all the questions; the snide remarks and the girlfriend business back at home.

Princess eased out of there quietly and walked to the front of the building, where a group of girls were waiting. Within seconds Mrs. Hinckly buzzed them in. The study lounge was still open, a place to calm her nerves before having to face Sherita in her suite. As painful as it was to think of Terry and Sherita as a couple, she had to face it. Whatever the story was, she wanted to hear it from Terry.

THREE MISERABLE days had passed and Princess had not breathed a word about what she'd heard. Her aloofness was so perceptible that Sherita didn't dare approach her and she avoided Terry at all costs. Having little appetite, Princess skipped dinner and decided to spend the time studying in the lounge. Immersed in her work, time almost slipped away.

"Shoot, it's nine-twelve!" Princess said, looking at her watch. *Curfew.* She quickly packed up her books, ran down to the laundry room and grabbed the remaining garments from the dryer and headed upstairs.

"Bonjour. Je m'appelle Princess. Comment t'appelles tu?" she repeated to herself, spelling the words in her mind as she walked through the corridor. *Another major French test. This teacher needs to slow it down in my opinion. I'll have to get up before breakfast and study some more.*

The second floor smelled of microwave popcorn, hairspray and fingernail polish. *American Idol* was on and had the floor's attention in the last minutes before curfew. All the girls, dressed in pajamas and robes, watched in awestruck intensity.

"Phone for Sherita. It's Corvette," yelled one of the girls.

Au jardin, la tulipe, la jacinthe, les marguerites, la rose—"

When Sherita rushed past her, she didn't acknowledge her whatsoever. Thirsty, Princess stopped at the water fountain for a cold drink. When she arrived at Suite 210 she found the door shut tight.

"Open up," she blared, knocking and turning the knob simultaneously. It was locked from the inside. "C'mon, it's Princess."

A portion of Snoopy's face appeared as the door was cracked open. "Why's the door locked?"

"You alone?" Snoopy asked, darting her eyes in all directions. She swung the door open and closed it quickly. Tyler was standing by the window with a ghostly look about her.

"What's going on?"

"I don't see her yet," Tyler uttered, terrified, not responding to the question but talking to the situation. "We've got to figure something out."

Princess released an exasperating sigh. "Oh, come on. Don't tell me."

"Be quiet!" ordered Saba. She was wearing a bright, knee-length T-shirt with the word 'Destined' written on it.

"If the lights are already out, Ms. Morgan won't know," Tyler suggested.

"But what if she turns them on and Stephanie's not here?" asked Snoopy.

"Not again," uttered Princess, annoyed. *This is not happening again. That's it. Stephanie's done! And we are about to be done as well if we get caught trying to cover for her.* "I can't believe that she—"

"Shut up! Quick, let's rearrange her bed," Tyler instructed. "Ms. Morgan won't be able to tell it's not her in the dark."

Saba pulled back the covers and threw a couple of karate chops to the pillow. Tyler went to her closet and pulled out her laundry bag full of clothes and put it on the bed. Snoopy snatched the scarf off her head and wrapped it neatly around a sweater and positioned it on the pillow.

"We need some more clothes," Saba said, running to the closet. "I can't get this combination working," she squealed, desperately pulling on the locks.

"Take some of mine," Snoopy offered, pointing to her open closet.

"Here, take this, too," Princess said, adding as much as she could to help make for a more authentic-looking dummy.

Snoopy hit the lights to test the look. The minutes were flying. Everyone got into their beds and pulled the covers over their shoulders in sheer fear.

"Be quiet, everybody, and listen for the window," Tyler told them.

Before Princess realized it, she had taken part in a conspiracy. They all had.

"What if she comes through the door with Ms. Morgan?" Snoopy asked Tyler.

"She won't, because she told me she was coming in and to watch for her at the back door. But when security locked the doors at nine, what could I do?" Tyler explained. "I couldn't wait."

"But why isn't she here yet?" Snoopy whispered.

"Who knows . . . lost track of time?" said Tyler

"Maybe she fell and broke her leg—

"This is scary," Princess quivered, cutting Saba off.

"It'll be even scarier if Stephanie gets caught," added Snoopy. "And we can't keep lying for her like this."

We don't live this dangerously in Telham Park, Princess thought What if Stephanie gets caught or, worse yet, gets hurt climbing up the building? How could I tell my family I'm being expelled or kicked out because I conspired with my suitemate's wrongdoing? The 'what if's' were looming large and coming fast.

"Wait a minute," Saba's voice rose up. "What if Stephanie came up with another story and Ms. Morgan already knows she's not here? What's she gonna say when she sees what looks like a person in the bed? She'll know we did it."

"She can't prove that," argued Tyler. "She left her clothes on her bed preparing them for laundry tomorrow and her books were left there, too. It's just a coincidence that her bed looks like a body is in it."

"Or maybe she came in earlier and set the whole thing up herself," Saba spoke out of imagination, in her attempt to create a believable story.

The door suddenly opened and the lights were turned on. "How come the lights are out already?" Sherita complained, entering the room. "We still have eight minutes." She looked over at Stephanie's bed and shook her head. "Still not here, huh?"

"Hurry up and get in bed," Saba pressed, more like insisted.

"Excuse you!" protested Sherita.

"Please, just turn off the lights," urged Tyler. "We don't want Ms. Morgan to be able to see in here."

The clock read nine-twenty-eight. The muffled sound of deep, heavy voices on walkie-talkie radios interrupted the usual quiet on the floor.

"You hear that?" Snoopy whispered. "Oh my God, they got her."

"Don't say that," advised Tyler.

"Where's Ms. Morgan?" Saba asked. "I don't hear her."

Tyler jumped up and felt her way to the door to listen. "Me either. Maybe she's got Stephanie."

In the silence came a continuing wheezing shrill. Princess was struggling to breathe. *Oh, God, I can't be having an asthma attack. Please not now.* Her inhaler was in her nightstand drawer but she didn't want to have to reach for it. *It'll pass . . . I hope.*

"You okay, Princess?" asked Snoopy.

"Yes."

Listening for Ms. Morgan on one end and listening out for Stephanie on the other was torture.

At nine-thirty-six, there was a knock on the door. Everybody froze. Princess' heart was pounding so hard she could feel her pulse in her head. She inhaled short quick breaths through her mouth and seconds later the door opened.

"Lights out!" said Ms. Morgan. The corridor light lit up most of the room as they all pretended to be sleep. "Very good, ladies."

Only the door didn't close. Princess opened one eye, watching Ms. Morgan tiptoeing down the center aisle to do a bed check.

"My stomach," Saba cried as she tore back the covers. "It hurts."

"Shhhh!" Ms. Morgan hushed her. "What's the matter?"

"I don't know, I have these bad cramps. Oh, God!"

"Have you eaten today?

"Um huh."

"In the cafeteria?"

"Yes."

"Could be having a reaction to something," Ms. Morgan muttered. "Hold on to me," she said and ushered a moaning Saba out of the room.

"No she didn't," Snoopy whispered incredulously.

"We were dead!" exclaimed Tyler. "Ms. Morgan was headed to Stephanie's bed."

"I know because she checked *me*," said Snoopy. "I felt her hand touch the bed."

Princess reached for her inhaler. Her wheezing was now audible. Snoopy jumped out of her bed. "Princess!"

Tyler jumped out of her bed and turned on the night lamp. "You okay?"

After two inhales from the pump, Princess was fine. "She touched me, too," Princess said, relieved now that she had regained control of her breathing.

"This is too much," Snoopy declared, holding her head in her hand. "Princess could've had an attack and started turning blue. Since the lights were out, we wouldn't have noticed and she could have been slowly dying right here in this room and by the morning she could have been—or what if we would have had to take her to the hospital and the paramedics didn't show up in time and Ms. Morgan—"

"Nothing like that would have happened," Tyler said, dismissing Snoopy's melodramatic monologue. "Princess is a trooper, right?"

"Uh huh."

Tyler felt Princess' forehead and neck and lightly massaged her head.

When the girls were certain Princess was all right Tyler and Snoopy returned to their beds and turned off the light.

Some thirty minutes later the door quietly opened. Everyone lay still, pretending to be sleep.

"Good night, Ms. Morgan."

"Good night."

"Hey!" Saba whispered. "Is she here yet?"

Everybody sat up except Sherita. She hadn't spoken a word throughout the whole ordeal.

"No," answered Tyler. "Does anybody know anything out there?"

"No, but somebody reported a possible intruder on the grounds, and security is searching all the dorms."

"Are you serious?" Snoopy whispered, terrified. "What if that's Stephanie and they see her and they pull their weapons and—"

"Would you shut up!" Saba exclaimed, climbing into bed. "It's after ten o'clock and she's not here. What are we going to do?"

"What can we do?" asked Tyler.

"If it gets too late, we're gonna have to say something," Princess mumbled. "What if she's in trouble?"

There were no more words. They fell back in their beds with scared thoughts and silent prayers.

At ten-seventeen, they heard a familiar sharp tapping at the window.

"What was that?" Tyler raised up, groping for an answer.

"I dunno," said Snoopy. "You think it's Stephanie?"

When they heard it again, Tyler jumped out of her bed, gently raised the blinds, opened the window and leaned out. Saba, Snoopy and Princess followed her. There was Stephanie down below, waving frantically.

"She's coming up," whispered Tyler.

Princess clutched Saba's hand. *Oh, God, please let this poor, pitiful child, who has no idea what she's doing, make it up here one last time without falling.*

With record speed, Stephanie's hands were grabbing the ledge of the windowsill and everybody moved to help pull her in.

"You're dead!" Saba chided.

"Did she call lights out already?" Stephanie sounded scared.

"You think she was waiting for you to climb through the window?" replied Saba. "Of course she did."

"Does she know I wasn't here?"

"No. Did anybody see you?" asked Tyler.

"No. No."

"We had you covered here," Saba told her.

Relieved, Stephanie exhaled heavily, feeling relief wash over her as she disrobed. She felt her way to her bed and fell on top of the buried clothes. "What's all of this?"

"Your clone," Tyler replied facetiously.

"Good thinking," she said, finding her way comfortably. "I love y'all . . . love y'all to death."

"Yeah, well, we don't love you for what you just put us through," Snoopy said. "And you almost made Princess have an asthma attack."

"Princess . . . Princess you okay?"

"Now that you're in this room I am." Princess was in post-shock mode. "I think you're losin' your mind."

"What kind of guy lets his girl climb up the side of a building?" Sherita's cutting comment drew everyone's attention to her.

"The kind of guy you wish you had," Stephanie snapped back. "You don't know what happened, so mind your business."

"I can just imagine," Sherita quipped sarcastically.

"Where in the world were you?" Tyler probed.

"I'm sorry," Stephanie apologized, switching gears. "For real, I'm sorry. But one thing's for sure. Suite 210 is the best suite in the house, yo!" She began quietly laughing.

"Right," Snoopy agreed, snickering. "This is a waiting-to-exhale moment."

"Last time, Stephanie," Tyler admonished. "I'm not kidding."

"Is it worth risking your track scholarship for?" Saba asked.

"Shhhh. You never know who's listening," said Stephanie, avoiding the question. "I'm going to sleep now."

Snoopy found the ordeal funny and surrendered to the comedy. "This is the life," she said, launching into a fit of laughter. "If our parents only knew." She laughed long and hard, though they all knew it was nervous laughter.

"You keep messing around like this Stephanie, ain't gonna be no life—all jokes aside," Princess advised, but then was bit by the contagious laughter.

Saba and Tyler also realized the humor in the potential tragedy and laughed themselves silly. It relieved Stephanie's tension, pulling her into it as well, and slowly relaxed their frazzled nerves. It took hours to wind down and for everyone to find sleep.

"WHERE YOU been, girl?" Terry asked, sitting next to Princess in the dining hall with a tray full of food.

Princess wanted to tell him where to go or abruptly leave, but she had been looking forward to a good meal all day. Staring blankly at him, she replied, "Busy."

The dinner hour was drawing to a close and the cafeteria was a quiet, long maze of dining tables. "Wanna tell me what's wrong?"

"Who said something was wrong?"

"Because you're not talking to me, not answering my calls . . . or my texts. Because I've been looking for you for four, five days now and nobody knows where you are.

You're not even lookin' at me now, so I know something's wrong." Terry cut into his meatloaf and wolfed down a big chunk.

Princess couldn't resist the opportunity to confront him. "Have you been honest with me?"

"Honest?" Terry cocked his head thoughtfully. "Straight-up honest. Why you ask me that?"

"What's going on with you and Sherita?"

Terry's jaws stopped moving suddenly. "Why? What did she tell you?" He had an uneasy look about him.

"She didn't tell me anything. She doesn't have to. But you do."

Terry continued to chew his food and fixed his gaze on the salt and pepper shakers in front of him.

"You got some kind of history with her?"

"I told you we grew up together. Been knowing her most of my life."

"So what was the conversation about?"

"What are talking about?"

"The one you recently had with her." Princess wouldn't say how she knew and he didn't ask.

Terry took a big gulp of cranberry juice and passed his napkin over his mouth. "Every time she sees me she's trying to get me to do something to get Blair's attention. I get tired of that, and I told her straight up."

"Is that all it is?"

"That's enough. The girl stalks Blair ridiculously and she wants me to do her dirty work. I'm not her messenger."

This is either an award-winning acting performance or he's telling the truth. "So why's she looking for you to hook her up?"

Terry chewed quickly and then swallowed. " 'Cause she knows me . . . and we play on the same team."

Princess turned and glanced at him. *Nuh uh, there's got to be more to it than this?*

"That's what's been on your mind?"

"Don't you think I needed to know?"

"You're coming to the game on Founder's Day, right?"

"And what about this girlfriend of yours?" Princess asked, ignoring his attempt to change the subject.

"What girlfriend?"

"The one she keeps telling everybody you have at home."

"You gotta understand her. Sherita's imagination works . . . I don't know, in some other frequency. I don't know nothin' about anybody else. I'm only concerned with the person sitting next to me."

Princess paused, remembering a task, and mentally added it to her 'To Do List.' Then decided to take him on his word . . . for now.

ten

"I'm definitely going to graduate school, law school, medical school or one of them," said Stephanie, joining Princess on the campus, following the Saturday morning Chapel assembly on Founder's Day. "Anywhere beyond the undergraduate level."

"Oh, no doubt. We would be crazy not to when they're offering us full fellowships," Princess pointed out. "That little old man was so sweet, wasn't he?"

"Well, when you're *that* rich, what other way is there to be?" sidelined Stephanie. "What does he own, like five franchises."

Princess had the opportunity to meet and speak with some of Boravia's older alumni at breakfast earlier. The wealthy men who became entrepreneurs, corporate CEO's, engineers, architects, doctors and lawyers expressed their promise of benevolence in exchange for continued excellence. As far as she was concerned, college couldn't come soon enough.

Mission accomplished for Alphonse Boravia, the American philanthropist. The boarding school was created for poor, white male orphans endowed from his immense fortune back in the 1800s. When he died, it was his wish to provide every advantage for future generations to live and learn without limits—like children of the privileged class—and not suffer the indignities that he had experienced as an orphan. But in the next century, during the late seventies, civil rights groups protested the strict admissions policy. Their efforts led to a diversified mix of enrollees in recent years, and a gradual sprinkling of minorities, both male and female.

This would have been the perfect time to have my family and Nadira come down here, Princess thought. I gotta admit I'm kinda proud to be a Boravian with all its advantages right at my fingertips. And now that I know Terry, it's all good. For sure my family will be here next year.

Horse-drawn carriages trotted throughout the campus carrying students, parents, and other visitors to food stations and other activities. All the barbecue, popcorn, cotton candy and drinks one could devour was set up and the lines were growing everywhere. The charcoal-broiled burgers looked scrumptious to Stephanie and Princess for starters, bypassing the cold food, Luigi's Italian buffet—filled with pastas and salads and dessert—and other international themed stations.

"I would've invited my family up here if I had known it was gonna be like this," Princess said, sinking her teeth into a burger.

"That's exactly why I didn't invite my parents," admitted Stephanie. "They would've been smothering me, trying to get all up in my business and I'da had to turn into Sister Corrina for the day."

"Whose that?"

"My alter ego when I'm home . . . and the daughter my parents want me to be."

"I thought your people were cool."

"The religious, sanctified ones? They'd be checking into everything and talking to everyone about me."

"And with Sherita around they wouldn't have to go too far."

"That's right, and I can't take those kinds of chances."

"I haven't seen her all day," Princess realized.

"She'll show up at the game 'cause she's gotta keep an eye on you and Terry." Stephanie teased. "But if she knows like I know, she'd better back off. I'll have her sweatin' like Susan."

"Who?"

"Susan Capps, the girl on the track team. You should have seen her in Chapel this morning."

"What happened?"

"She was sweatin' like a pig. Scared to death."

"Scared of what?"

"I heard she was hangin' with that wrestler. You know, that big dude who walks like *Ah-nuld*."

"They call him Tank?"

"Yeah, that's him. All of sudden, she's been missing practice lately, right."

"She doesn't want to run anymore?"

"No. I think she's sick and she *can't* run."

"Get out!" Princess exclaimed, pushing Stephanie so hard her burger almost slipped. "You don't think she's pregnant?"

Stephanie laughed at Princess' astonishment. "I think I do. When the speaker was talking about morals and values and a strict code of ethics this morning, girlfriend couldn't sit still."

"And if she is, she's out, right?"

"Off the team, yeah—and out of the school, too!"

Chills ran through Princess at the thought of such expulsion. *Your whole life ruined, just like that.* "Stephanie, you gotta be more careful, I'm serious. No more spidergirl acts, cuz if you ever get caught—"

"Nnnnot gonna happen."

"Anything's possible when you're taking chances like that." Worry surfaced in Princess' eyes. "Think they'll let her finish the semester?"

"Yeah . . . if they don't know about it." Stephanie looked intently at Princess. "She would only be a few months by then anyway, so unless she told the school, they would never know. Especially if she decided to make it disappear, know what I'm sayin'?"

"Uh huh."

"Technically though, according to the rules, she would be out for having sex and getting pregnant, regardless of what she decided to do about it. 'Cause Boravians are not supposed to be indulging in such activity."

"*Riiiight!* What planet are these people livin' on?" Princess smirked.

"But it's all good for them 'cause you know how rich people wash their dirty laundry. There'll be some family emergency in Switzerland somewhere all of a sudden, and she'll have to leave school for a minute. Come back here the next week with some nice little story and everything will be cool."

"Huh, wouldn't be like that if it were one of us."

"Tell it like it *tis*, sistah."

"We would be out before the home pregnancy test could turn pink or blue or however it goes," Princess said.

They laughed at the threat of expulsion from Boravia, only they secretly shared in the terror of the possibility. "Can you picture that?" asked Stephanie looking lost in a thousand-yard stare. "Going back home to our 'not so affluent' neighborhoods, pretending we didn't like it here, but the truth of the matter is, we didn't live up to their expectations. I can hear them now. 'Poor little black teenagers. We tried to give them an opportunity. They just don't measure up. They're better off in their own communities.' Hypocrites!"

"You know it."

Stephanie trashed her napkin and went for a soda. "It's time for me to get outta here. I'll catch up to you at the game."

"Alright, later." Princess looked around and spotted the procession of horses galloping through the campus, wishing she were one of the riders. The she recognized Satin, all dressed up and looking clean. For the experience, she decided to stand on line for the horse-and-buggy tour.

IN THE BLINK of an eye the afternoon shot by and before Princess knew it, she and Snoopy were seated in the Armory, watching the game. The slam-dunk win for the current Warriors lineup wasn't as easy as they had anticipated and they were hard at work for a win. At halftime, the cheerleaders entertained the audience with their choreographed dance moves that could be described with one phrase. *A hot mess!* Princess shook her head, grunting in contempt while watching them perform.

"Look at that!" Snoopy lamented. We could do better than that on a bad day."

"Eyes closed and everything," agreed Princess. It was true. The girls' moves were stale, predictable, and had no uplifting powers. "Couldn't raise the spirit of a fly with what they're doing out there."

"What they really need is a cross between some cheerleadin' and some steppin' . . . with some sistazs doin' it, of course," said Snoopy. "Call it the zebra effect."

"There you go!"

"We're waitin' on you to get it started," said Snoopy.

"Me?"

"You're the only one up here who knows how to step. Get you a group and get started."

"With all the work I have to do . . . I don't know about that."

"It's always the busy people that make things happen, don't you know that. C'mon, let's get something to drink."

"No, I'm good."

"Just a little something?" Snoopy, looking around anxiously. "I have to go to the bathroom, too. And while I do that, you can stand on the food line for me. It won't take long . . . please?"

"What would you do if I weren't – alright."

Snoopy huddled closely to Princess as they slowly made their way through the crowd.

"Princess, look, there they are."

"Who?"

"Langsford's parents. I met them earlier. Whatchu think?"

"About what?"

"What kind of people do you think they are?"

"I can't tell anything by just *looking* at them . . . and what am I s'pose to be looking for?"

"I don't know, they might be racist . . . or do you think they like me?"

"Like I can read that on their faces? Besides, the ones that smile in your face are the worst ones."

"Look again."

"I don't know. They look like normal people. I mean, when he introduced you to them, what did he introduce you as?"

"As Charity."

"And so . . . what was their reaction?"

"They just kinda smiled . . . like white people do."

"No, but do you think they think something's up? I mean why's Langsford introducing his parents to this African American girl?"

"As a friend."

"Maybe that's why you didn't get any reaction. They're not taking y'all seriously . . . and why should they?"

"True, dat."

Princess glanced around, keeping all the different people in her radar. "They probably feel the same way your parents would feel in the same situation."

"My mother could probably live with it, but I know my dad would flip. Shoot, and he graduated from Howard, too. He's expecting me to come home one day with a tall, chocolate-covered medical student, well-spoken, with good manners and hungry for his baby girl."

"For real?"

"Well, he and all his friends are doctors, so you know he's already got one of their sons matched up with me in his mind."

"I didn't know your father was a doctor!"

"Yep. An oncologist."

"So he treats people with tumors and different kinds of cancer."

"Smart girl. Most people can't even pronounce the word."

"All this time and you never told me. I don't believe you. So that's where you get your brains from?"

"What! My mother's smarter than he is all day long, shooooot."

"So you're gettin' the brains from both ends."

"Yeah, but my mother and father are divorced so I've got two separate homes to live in and two personalities to deal with—and they're totally opposite."

"You have sisters and brothers?"

"Nope."

"So whose idea was it for you to come to Boravia?"

"My mother's. Guess she needed some space. She's on a mission with all these women causes in third world countries."

As they walked, it struck Princess strange that Snoopy lived among the so-called upper-middle-class and might even be rich. Even so, she was so nice, unpretentious and seemingly unspoiled.

"Whoa, maybe I'm not that thirsty," Snoopy remarked, looking at the long beverage line. They suddenly stopped, trading wild stares at one another.

"Get some ice cream instead or something. That line is shorter over there," Princess suggested.

"No, I really wanted something to drink."

"My guess is the line in the bathroom is probably just as long. You gotta go that bad?"

"Sure do."

"Well, you go on and I'll stand on this line here." Princess had never seen the Armory so crowded. Traffic was snarled in both directions and people were crammed together.

"Princess!" Someone called out of the crowd.

She looked behind her and saw Sherita waving energetically, which struck her as odd.

"Standing in line?" she asked as she and a friend inched closer.

"For a minute, yeah." Princess response was dry and distant.

"What's up with you? Oh! Did you meet Corvette?"

"No I didn't," Princess replied, turning to Corvette and switching gears to a more pleasant demeanor. "How you doin'?"

"Nice to meet you."

Big-boned and voluptuous, she was the same height as Sherita with beautiful brown eyes and perfect carnation-toned skin. Her hair weave looked wet and seductive, and her make-up was piled on thick.

"You're visiting?" Princess asked, taking note of her tightly fitted jeans and her fuchsia-colored boots that matched her sweater.

"Yeah, just for the day."

"Princess, Corvette's from the Palisades, where I live."

"Oh, really? That's good. Hope you have a good time here."

"That's an understatement. Terry's got her day worked out for her," said Sherita.

"Huh?" Princess looked oddly at her as if she had heard her incorrectly. She tried to keep her pleasant, social face intact.

"Corvette's Terry's friend, the one I told you about. He invited her here."

"Oh . . . okay," Princess said faintly, drawing up a pretentious smile.

"We're going to the locker room to see him now." The two had been stalling the line of traffic behind them and had to move along.

"Nice to meet you, Princess."

"Um yeah, nice meeting you, too." Princess never looked at her again and she had no conscious idea of what she had said. *It was all a lie! He does have a girlfriend and then had the audacity to invite her here. What did he think, I wouldn't see her? Tell me this isn't happening. Corvette's being escorted around campus by Sherita as Terry's girlfriend. Me, the one with the 'Small Talk' column. Now the small talk is gonna be about me.*

Princess felt as if her clothes were peeling off of her little by little and she would soon be exposed for the world to see. She wanted to run but she couldn't in the crowded area. Nausea crept into her stomach. Little hot pins jabbed at her and she felt faint as she shoved her way to the nearest exit door.

"Princess! Princess!" A frantic cry came out of the circle of noise.

Distraught, Princess never turned around and ran back to Bryant Hall with her thoughts fixed on going back home to Telham Park. By the time she'd reached the stairwell at Bryant, her tears were falling uncontrollably. Fearing someone might be in her room and see her, she slowed down and sat in the corner of the top stair and drew her knees to her chest.

The betrayal caused her to recollect other dark moments in her life when she had been let down. Nothing could have been worse than her father's conscious absence from her life. The denial of his active parenting left her heart with an aching, gaping hole. Those long moments anticipating his arrival on Saturdays to pick her up, as the custody agreement had stated, resulted in pure disillusionment. She negotiated different scenarios in her mind while watching Saturday morning cartoons, hoping he'd show up. He'll be here after *The Jetsons*, she thought. Then *The Flintstones* came on. Okay, I'll watch *Scooby Doo* and give him a little more time, she recalled. By the time *Soul Train* was over at noon and he didn't call, her heart grew heavy and a cold emptiness set in. To distract the hurt, she would help her mother with house chores or write her feelings in her diary. Consumed by these sad memories, she hardly heard the thumping of feet coming up the stairs.

"Princess! Princess! What's wrong?" It was Snoopy.

Princess turned her face away and tried to cover her eyes. "Nothing."

Snoopy forced Princess' hands away from her face. "You're crying! What's the matter? Why did you leave like that?"

"I had to get out of there."

"Why?" Snoopy pleaded, sitting on the steps next to her.

Princess buried her head into her folded arms and cried.

"C'mon Princess, tell me. What's wrong?" Snoopy tried to force her arms open.

"Somebody said something to you . . . what?" She was scared for Princess.

"He's a liar!" Princess fired out, her eyes a bloodshot red.

"Who?"

"Terry."

"What did he do?"

Princess paused, cradling her wounded spirit and allowing a fresh rush of tears to roll down her cheeks.

"Here, take these," Snoopy said, handing Princess some tissues from her pocket. "Okay, now tell me what happened."

Princess pulled herself together and began to speak between sniffles. "When I was . . . waiting for you . . . Sherita came over to me . . . with Terry's girlfriend."

"Terry doesn't have a girlfriend!"

"At home he does . . . and he invited her to the game."

Snoopy's eyes grew large with disbelief.

"Sherita comes up to me talkin' like everything's cool . . . which I thought was strange 'cause . . . you know she hasn't said much to me in weeks . . . and I'm just talkin' to the girl . . . and then . . . she says, 'This is Terry's girlfriend.' "

"You lyin'!"

"Well, she didn't exactly call her his girlfriend but . . . she said Terry invited her here."

"Maybe they're just friends. I can't believe Terry would do something like that. I mean, he knows you were gonna see her or somebody was gonna tell you about her. But why would he—"

"I don't know," Princess sobbed. "She didn't look like a *friend* to me. . . . Do you know how embarrassed I was?"

"Wait a minute, stop crying. Okay . . . tell me . . . what did this girl look like?"

"Kinda tan . . . big eyes, wearin' this triflin' weave . . . sorta cute."

"So you think she's—

"Yes!"

"No, I'm not havin' it," Snoopy said, rising up. "Let's go find him and straighten this out right now."

"No! I don't want to see him," Princess cried forcing her back down.

"Yeah, but he can't get away with this. Somebody needs to tell him what—"

"That's not gonna change anything. I'm gonna be the one looking stupid. Plus—" Princess paused and cleared her throat. "I don't want anybody to know I could be played like that. Sherita said he had a girlfriend, but I didn't believe it. Nobody did."

"You're not stupid. He's the stupid one. The balls of this *freakin'* . . . and I thought he was cool. Anytime you think you can screw people around, especially somebody like you. I can't wait to see him."

Princess could feel her tears returning, and threw her face into the palms of her hands.

"Don't cry Princess, please," Snoopy said, hugging her friend and fighting off her own tears. "He's gonna get his, you watch."

"Don't tell anybody, please," Princess pleaded. "Just . . . I don't want anyone to know, leave it alone. I'll be alright."

"This just doesn't sound right to me. Are you sure you got a good reading on this?"

"That's his girlfriend, I'm telling you."

"Okay, okay," Snoopy said. Tightly she pursed her lips and squinted her eyes, not yet convinced. "I'm gonna find out the real story, you'll see."

"Just drop it. Snoopy, I'm serious.

"Okay, okay."

"But I'll never say anything to him again." Princess rubbed the earring she was wearing that Terry had given her. "Can you . . . would you go and see if anybody's in the room? I want to go lie down."

"Of course I will," Snoopy replied. "Of course."

From: "Princess Brixton"
To: "Nadira Watford"
Subject: Troubled

Nadira,

I hate this place! Terry tried to make a fool out of me. Remember I told you about my suitemate who was trying to tell me that Terry had a girlfriend? I asked him, to his face, and all he kept saying was no, no, no. Well, guess who just happens to pop up at the game on Founder's Day? I wish you would have been there 'cause I thought I was gonna go mad! Now there I am standing there, looking like an idiot and making some small talk about God knows what. Come to find out she's Terry's girlfriend. You don't know, I wanted to die! Can you believe he did this to me? I felt like the whole world was laughing at me. Now he's chasing after me, but I never want to see or speak to him, ever again! I think it's time for me to come back to Telham Park and re-think my decision about Boravia. Holla back!

LYLAS

THE DEADLINE for 'Small Talk' selections for the next issue of *The Boravia Communicator* was only days away. In the newspaper office Princess worked diligently, sifting through letters and e-mails, pulling out only those that sparked her interest. No, no, not this one. *No, no . . . okay maybe.* Two students wanted to announce their intent to market a new kind of soft pretzel. *No way. I can't do that one here.*

Internet Romance. *Hmmm, this is gold. But how come I haven't heard from her?* Princess had e-mailed the writer several days before requesting additional information and never received a response. *Let me check my e-mail again.*

Princess turned to Julia, one of the general assignment reporters, for help. "What do you do when you're trying to e-mail a student and they don't respond?"

"Move on to the next story," she teased.

"No, but I want this one. It's pretty good."

"Hmmm, maybe you can find out who it is from the address."

"Okay, her address is ELCEE."

Julia wrapped her lengthy brown hair around her ear and examined the information through her square-rimmed glasses. She was a soft-spoken, intellectual geek from whom almost everyone sought information. "Um nope, doesn't sound familiar," she said. "Look it up in the school roster and see if you get a match for that name. Try first names and last names. Oh, and look up middle names or initials."

After exhausting all options, Princess sat at her desk, lost in thought, drawing doodles around the address. Re-examining the address closely, she scrambled the letters, spelled the address backward, and then decided to separate the word into syllables. ELCEE could be the spelling for the initials LC. She thought it was a long shot, but she wanted to see who owned those initials. Back to the roster she went.

Five names fit those initials and two of them were boys. That narrowed the choices. Whoever this person was had to be an upperclassman because she spoke about a weekend pass. Two of the girls were freshman class leaving only one possible candidate.

"Apologies, Julia, but I gotta interrupt you again. Do you know a girl by the name of Lisa Capote?"

"Of course, everybody does. She's the girl that was attacked two weekends ago. Why?"

"Just something I saw her name on," Princess said coolly, showing no expression.

This is too strange of a coincidence. ELCEE had been so excited about meeting her soul mate on her next weekend pass and then the attack happened. That is, if this is the same person. I'm still not sure. Princess' mind shifted into overdrive. Flashes of violence appeared again in her head. Lisa Capote dreams of Internet romance, asks for a weekend pass, and then gets attacked. *Could this be the same girl?*

Throughout the evening, Princess couldn't shake her uneasiness about her suspicions. In the silence of the night she wondered if she had stumbled on to clues leading to Lisa's attacker. She was even haunted by it as she slept, tossing, and turning, contemplating what to do. The next morning, sleepy but confident, she decided to share her thoughts with school officials.

"YOU MEAN to tell me that someone named ELCEE told you she was meeting this young man on a weekend pass?" Mrs. DeMarco asked, snatching her bifocals off. It was quiet in the newspaper office in the morning and the two of them were alone.

"I wanted to run her story in this issue, so I e-mailed her with some questions. She hasn't responded since that weekend. I could be wrong, but it seems to be a spooky coincidence."

"Yes, it does," Mrs. DeMarco said, looking troubled.

"I have a print-out of the e-mail right here," Princess said, leading Mrs. DeMarco to her workstation. "I'm just not sure about who this ELCEE is"

Mrs. DeMarco mumbled as she read the e-mail. She drew a deep breath, sighed dramatically and said, "I think we have to run with this. The worst that can happen is we followed up a wrong lead, and right now we don't have any others. If ELCEE is Lisa Capote, then we need to find out who her so-called soul mate is."

"How can we get into her e-mail?"

"Just ask her. If this is the man that attacked her, wouldn't you think she'd want to know?"

"But this was confidential information. How is she gonna feel—"

"Princess, sweetie, this information could possibly save someone's life. Thank God Lisa is okay. But what if this guy is some kind of serial rapist or murderer?"

Princess clasped her hand and held it to her chest. You think he's—"

"Maybe Lisa didn't think of it, either. Or maybe she's scared and doesn't want the school to know . . . or her family."

"But wouldn't it be . . . a natural suspicion?" Princess asked. "You plan to meet your mystery date and somebody attacks you."

"Not necessarily. Remember, this wasn't a solo plan. She was with a group; she had to be in order to get a weekend pass. But then again . . . maybe that's why she slipped away. Because you know they found her in the upper deck of the parking lot."

"Parking lot?" *I saw something like that . . . in a dream or—*"

"Said she wanted to put her packages in the trunk before the movie started," Mrs. DeMarco continued. "One of the girls had a friend up for the weekend who had driven them to the mall. I mean, why only her? Could she have been sneaking out to meet this man or maybe got caught in the wrong place at the wrong time and it's purely a coincidence?"

"Can she identify him?"

"From what I was told, he attacked her from the back and tried to cover her mouth with a cloth, probably with chloroform on it, but she fought him like a wild animal. That's where all of her bruises came from."

"My God!"

"Don't worry, Princess. I'll handle it from here. You just continue your work, sweetie. That reminds me, there was a letter left on my desk for 'Small Talk.'"

On the way out, Princess stopped at her workstation to read the letter. It said:

A spidergirl is on the loose. She and her boyfriend, the basketball champ, get so busy sometimes they lose track of time (no pun intended). She's a track athlete, by the way, who sneaks in after curfew and climbs up the side of her building.

If you want to catch a glimpse of her, look out the back side of Bryant Hall facing east after lights out on Sunday nights—oh, and be on the lookout on Wednesdays also.

Princess gasped, dropping the note as if it were on fire. *Somebody knows, or maybe a lot of people know. Who told them? Does Stephanie know that people know? I've gotta tell her so she can be prepared when the questions come. Thank God Mrs. DeMarco didn't see this!*

Math lab was the last class on Tuesdays. When the chapel bell sounded, Princess had her knapsack packed and was ready to jet. She didn't lag behind to compare quiz grades or chat with Malira as they usually did.

"Where you running off to?" asked Snoopy, chasing Princess out of the building.

"I've gotta find Stephanie."

"Why you walking that way?"

" 'Cause I'm going to the Armory to find her."

"No, they practice on the track after school."

"Oh," Princess said, stopping to change her course. Oddly, Snoopy stood in her path.

"Listen to this, Princess. I saw Terry at lunch, right. He's got this puppy dog look about him. He came over to me asking about you. And don't you know, Sherita came out of nowhere and jumped up in my face! Terry gave her this look that was lethal and walked away like he was disgusted."

"I don't care about that," Princess replied abruptly, beginning to walk.

"Yeah, but listen, I got to thinking," Snoopy said, grabbing Princess' arm. She was eager to expound on her point. "How come Terry always acts like that with her? Especially when they're supposed to be so cool. I mean, they come from the same neighborhood and everything, but they act real hostile with each other. I say something's up with them."

"That's their business."

"But Princess, it came back to me. When I was ushering on Founder's Day morning, I checked that girl Corvette in. She was Sherita's guest, not Terry's. It hit me like days later, so I checked it out."

"That's no news. They know each other from home."

"Yeah, but where have you heard that name Corvette before?"

"Other than the name of a car?"

"No! On the phone, remember? I answered the hall phone twice when she called for Sherita. So then it hit me. I think Sherita schemed this whole thing up."

Princess didn't react as she walked across the campus. "Okay, I could almost buy it, except for the fact that Sherita said Terry invited her here. Corvette smiled at me like it was the truth."

"Maybe Sherita told her that or . . . they could be in on this together," said Snoopy. "You know how friends do. C'mon, think. Why didn't she check in as Terry's guest instead of Sherita's?"

"At this point it doesn't even matter, Snoopy, 'cause I'm through with him anyway. Finished! Done!"

CAN SHE run or what? Stephanie's legs whirred like bicycle spokes as she sprinted around the track. She was the shortest one on the team, but per the statistics, the fastest. Princess dashed out to the damp field, waving to grab her attention, with Snoopy following her. Stephanie stopped immediately at the sight of them, sensing something was wrong. Princess took her aside, anxious to drop the bomb, and handed her the note. Through hard, panting breaths she read it.

"Mrs. DeMarco gave it to me right after we got caught up in this thing about Lisa."

"Lisa who?"

"The girl who was attacked. Long story, I'll tell you about it later. Anyway, we were so into that, she just handed me the note and didn't bother reading it because it was my department. But it had *her* name on it. I mean, everybody knows any news coming to 'Small Talk' should be addressed to me. So why would someone address this to Mrs. DeMarco?"

" 'Cause she's a snake, that's why. Didn't I tell you about Sherita?"

"You think it's from her?" asked Snoopy.

"Who else knows? You know Saba and Tyler didn't tell. Then there's us."

"So duplicitous!" cried Snoopy.

"Or maybe you did it?"

Snoopy's eyes flared at the insinuation. "I would never do something like that! C'mon, how could you even fathom such a ridiculous possibility? Because if anyone would ever do something like that to me I would probably—"

"I'm kidding," said Stephanie. "It's Sherita, I know it is. That's why she addressed the note to Mrs. DeMarco, 'cause she didn't want you to see it."

"And if Mrs. DeMarco had read it," Princess quickly rejoined, "there'd be some investigation and they would find out it's you."

"That's right."

"You could get kicked out of school for that," said Princess.

"What does she care? Then she wouldn't have to listen to me playing you up with Terry."

"That's a dead issue!"

"What you mean?" asked Stephanie.

"I'm not *ever* dealing with him again."

"Why not?"

Snoopy looked at Princess and anxiously mouthed, "Can I tell her?"

"I don't care," Princess nodded.

Snoopy quickly summarized the whole story.

"Oh!" said Stephanie mortified. "That's why you've been feeling different around here lately . . . but I agree with you, Snoopy. I'm not buyin' it. We don't know Terry that well, but he would have to be a fool to do something like that, Princess. I don't believe it, and I'm gonna ask Damien. He would know."

"Yeah but he's not gonna give up his friend."

"He don't have to give 'em up. I can tell if Damien's lying."

"Don't worry about that, Stephanie. It's squashed. I'm more concerned about this letter. 'Cause I may not be able to catch the next one that's delivered to Mrs. DeMarco."

The afternoon sun cast a shadow over Stephanie's face. She looked out at the field and said, "There won't be a next one. She wants to play with me like that, I got a little something for her." Stephanie drew her face back and arched her left eyebrow with a look of contempt that Princess had never seen before. She began to jog in place. This is between us, okay."

The girls shook their heads in compliance.

"Cool. We'll talk about it later, gotta run."

From: "Nadira Watford"
To: "Princess Brixton
Subject: Advice

Princess,

Relax. Take a deep breath. Now release it. Something's not right here. From all the things you told me about Terry, it doesn't work. But then again, he might be one of those dudes that don't have a conscience. If it's true—he's history! I say confront him and put it all on the table.

Your suitemate is a skeezer and can't be trusted. I mean, what does she call herself doing, spying on you for her girl? But then what kind of girl is this so-called girlfriend if she knows Terry's up there squeezing somebody else's fruit. I don't buy it because Sherita would have told her about you. She's lucky she's not in Telham Park. We don't play that here.

That's a small thing compared to the madness here. Remember Bobatunde, the brother from Nigeria selling the leather bags on the street? The cops mistook him for somebody else and shot him dead. They claim they thought he had a gun and he fit the description of a suspect they'd been looking for. Some white cops killed him like a dog, shot him over twenty times. They said they thought he was armed with a gun. Bobatunde had a Bible in his pocket. It's gotta end. We're all grieving for his family. It's partly our fault. Until we stand up and do something, I'm talking something 'out of the box,' nothing is gonna change.

I'll fill you in with the news as it comes. Everybody sends their love.

LYLAS

eleven

Princess plopped down in the leather chair and whirled around, scanning books and observing pictures of twentieth-century writers at the Literary Hop, a private lounge for reading enthusiasts, writers and book club members.

"Now this is comfort," she said with a satisfied smile. "I could fall asleep up in here."

Snoopy's relentless nagging had finally paid off. She had repeatedly asked Princess to join her for lunch at the collegiate den. They were holding a reading today for burgeoning authors, and Princess agreed to sit on the panel of critics and be a judge.

"You can take off your shoes if you want to," Snoopy told her. "And whip out some of those snacks you got. I brought some, too."

Princess sipped a brimming cup of hot chocolate and sighed happily. "Now I see why you live here."

"I tried to tell you."

"So how many books do you read a week?"

"Two to three."

"And pulling off A's at the same time, you must be a speed-reader."

"Girl, I get lost in books. Always loved to read. When everybody else is sleeping, I'm reading."

"And you're not on any teams or anything, so you don't have any real distractions."

Snoopy flashed Princess a naughty glance, referring to her new friendship. "Excuse me. No distractions? Look at this chessboard he gave me."

"Aww . . . that's so cute."

"See the chessmen . . . they're made out of stone-washed porcelain."

"So what does that mean . . . he's in love or somethin'?"

"I dunno," Snoopy cackled, "but these little pieces don't come cheap."

"Chess . . . I don't know . . . never got into it," Princess admitted.

"Me either, but I'm learning to like it."

"And him too, right?"

Snoopy shrugged. "He's cool . . . and so smart. Science fiction, sports, geology, computers, you name it, we can talk about it . . . even racism."

"How does he feel about it?"

Again she shrugged. "He knows it's real."

"Well, how does he feel about you and him? Is he the type to like . . . openly protest discrimination, or is he one of those who sit back and pretend the sun is shining when it's raining?"

"Hmmm . . . I don't know," Snoopy pondered and then decided to let it go. "C'mon, let me show you how to play."

"I'll take the black ones," said Princess, lining up the pieces.

"Okay. First of all you gotta know that chess is a mind game. You want to try to read your opponent's thoughts and get into their spirit. This way you can kinda like . . . seduce them into error."

"So you're saying you gotta trick them?"

"No, not trick them really, but— Okay, you observe them in the silence and put yourself in the opponent's shoes. You know, sorta like mental telepathy. See, you want to set 'em up so they'll miscalculate your intentions. Then they'll hurry up, move too quickly, make a mistake and then BAM! You got 'em."

"But I don't understand this game like I do checkers. Seems too complicated."

"Not really. It's just a challenge of the mind. Okay, look at it this way. The chessboard is like two states separated by a river. The river is the center of the board. And of course the people, who are the chessmen, want to cross over and get into the other state's territory."

"Sorta like how black and white folks do, right?"

Snoopy leaned back in open-mouthed laughter. "You stupid, Princess. Where'd you get that from?"

"That's the Brooklyn coming out in me."

"Okay, you want to make sure your pieces are strongest in the center," Snoopy continued. "Your king should be protected by a castle. That's when you want to move to the side and away from the center, and at the same time move the rook toward the center. Like this, the white pieces should be perfectly positioned and ready to move."

"So how does it feel?"

"What?"

"Hangin' with a white dude."

"Different . . . but I'm comfortable with Langsford."

Princess watched her hands moving the pawns.

"Now, the dream position takes ten moves."

"So what's gonna happen when he makes his moves on you?" Princess asked, gazing at Snoopy closely. "When he goes for the goods?"

Snoopy muffled her laughter, pounding the table. "Well, you know he asked me to go to the Social with him," she then said, straight-faced.

"Okay, so what are you going to do?"

Snoopy repositioned several pawns, thinking of the ideal moves, mumbling. "There's a hundred ways to go from here, but that's where the skills come in."

"Answer the question, please. Are you going with him or what?"

Snoopy paused briefly. "Nobody else asked me, so what am I supposed to do? Go alone?"

"Ay . . . remember what you told me? Don't worry 'bout who you love, worry 'bout who's lovin' you . . . even if he is vanilla."

Their two hands reached up and smacked together in a high-five.

"That's what I'm talkin' about," affirmed Snoopy. "C'mon, let me show you the rules. Oh, and we gotta eat. The reading starts in fifteen minutes."

WITH LESS than three weeks before the Millennium Social, Boravia's gossip sizzled and 'Small Talk's' message box was on fire. Sought-after eligibles were scarce for girls and the cat fighting had begun. They were stopping at nothing to win over their prey.

The long-stemmed red rose sat on the steps of Bryant Hall. It was the third one delivered this week for Sherita with an anonymous note attached.

"Princess, don't you think all these roses I've been receiving could be considered newsworthy?" she asked, entering the room following study period on a Tuesday. She kicked back on the bed with her nose nestled in the rose

"And what are you asking me for?" Princess replied, her focus glued to her locker.

"I kinda thought it would be a different twist to print a story about a girl being lavished with flowers by her secret admirer."

"There's a certain criteria for the stories I select," Princess told her.

"What makes you think somebody wants to read about you and your secret admirer?" Stephanie interjected boldly. She sat in the center of the floor, stretching to touch her toes.

"Nothing wrong with giving a girl her due when she's in demand," Sherita answered cockily, snickering as she continued to tickle her nose with the rose.

Princess closed her locker door and headed to the shower. "E-mail it to 'Small Talk' and it'll be reviewed with the others."

"Can't you just print it? Why should I have to compete with less important news?"

"Because that's the way it's done, that's why." *The audacity of this girl! She doesn't know she's playing with fire.*

"Maybe I'll just send it to Mrs. DeMarco and see what she thinks about it."

Stephanie and Princess threw knowing glances at each other. Now they were sure she'd sent the note exposing Stephanie's after-hours window antics.

Saba bolted through the door and swept past Princess, a trail of tobacco stench following her.

"Freakin' parents!"

"What's the matter?" Princess asked.

"They're like . . . from a different century. Can you picture me wearing this?" She testily displayed a magazine clipping of a long-sleeved, silk chiffon dress that buttoned to the neck with a big bow in the back. Princess and Stephanie examined it. "Go ahead, crack up. My parents have totally lost it!"

"They bought this for you?" Stephanie questioned, staring at the dress that was obviously so unbecoming of Saba.

"Not yet, but they wanted to know if I liked it."

"So just tell them."

"The problem is, they want her to wear what they like," Princess surmised.

"Get over it!" Saba snapped. "Do I look like I want to be Cinderella?"

"So what are you going to do?" probed Stephanie.

"I'm gonna call my step brother in San Francisco and ask his wife to send me what I want."

"Will she do it?" Princess asked.

"Yeah . . . I mean, why not? She works for *FashionDom*."

"The *magazine*?"

"Yeah, she's been there since she graduated from college," said Saba. "And designers are always sending them samples of their newest creations. You should see her wardrobe. All kinds of stuff, ya know . . . nice colors, simple, elegant, this century."

"I say do it," Stephanie said. "But how do you know—"

"Lemme see it," Sherita ordered, snatching the clipping from Stephanie's hand.

Stephanie snatched it back. "When I'm finished." And she continued. "At least you can tell your sister-in-law what to look for."

"It's not the worst I've ever seen," said Tyler, evaluating the picture. "To a stranger, it would work. To us it screams. We know you."

"And everybody else here does, too," agreed Saba. "That's the point."

Snoopy never said a word. She was reading.

"I'm taking my shower," said Princess, walking out abruptly.

Stephanie picked up her towel and wrapped it around her neck. "I'm right behind you."

OPEN MIKE night in the Fisher Room at the library was all that it had promised to be—a poetry slam that was an enjoyable diversion. The evening was still young when it ended, so Princess decided to go upstairs to continue her research for a history assignment. Among the fourth-floor stacks, she removed several books on the Cold War to examine them more closely.

"Psssst," came a noise, startling her. "Hey, girl. What's going on?"

Sandwiched between two rows of books was Terry's face. Princess sucked her teeth and turned away, annoyed.

His face fell at her cold refusal. Then he walked parallel to her and met her at the end of the stack. "What's the matter with you?"

Princess did an about-face and changed her direction to avoid him.

"Where you going?"

Princess weaved in and out of the students reading in the aisles. Quickly she walked down another artery of stacks to the very end and turned in the opposite direction.

"Princess," he called louder, distracting several students working nearby.

He'd better not make a scene in here 'cause I'll—"

"Princess," he called again, and she ripped down the aisle trying to go down to another floor. When she reached the exit door, Terry bumped into her head-on. "You gonna talk to me or what?"

Whichever direction Princess moved, he defensively blocked her.

"Get out of my way," she demanded coldly, refusing to make eye contact.

"When you explain yourself."

"You can't be serious!"

A student came through the door and Terry was forced to move. Princess took off, but Terry caught her by the arm.

"Get off me!"

"Not until we talk."

"I said get off of me!"

"Why don't you just let—"

To escape his grip, Princess threw a hard fist to his chest and ran down the stairs. *If he knows what I know, he'd better stay away from me.*

Terry followed her out onto the campus grounds. She walked as fast and as hard as she could but Terry, with his long, athletic strides, took one step to her every two.

"Princess, what do you want . . . you want me to beg you? Too many fish in the sea."

"Then start swimming, I don't care."

She walked past Rimpkin Hall, Founder's Hall, and cut through the Administration Building. As she struggled to stay ahead of him, she felt a familiar tightness in her chest. Large groups of students began making their way to and from the Armory, their voices lively in the onset of dusk.

"If you gonna kick a brother to the curb, you can at least tell him why," Terry argued, walking right next to her. "You're gonna go on like this forever or what . . . 'cause I'm not into chasing anybody."

"And neither am I!" Princess shot back. She was pissed at him. Mad for what she did and more angry at herself for falling prey to his schemes. Her chest felt heavy and her breathing was becoming more difficult. She slowed down out of necessity and looked at him, her eyes flashing with fury. "I don't know how y'all living down here, but where I come from . . . think you can play me like Chelsea plays that violin? And just in case you haven't noticed, I'm not starving for any attention. It could be you today, a real man tomorrow."

"What you talking about?" Terry piped. He looked confused.

"And I still have your earring. I'll send it to you in the mail."

"I don't want it back. I gave it to you." A throbbing ache needled at him as he watched Princess departing.

Her chest felt strangely tight, and she could hear herself wheezing. She stopped to try to regain her breath. Her backpack suddenly felt heavy, so she let it fall. Gasping for air, Princess grabbed her chest.

Catching a glimpse of her fear-struck eyes, Terry rushed over to her. "What's the matter?"

"Asthma," she rasped, her eyes softened in helplessness.

"You got your pump?" he asked, going for her bag.

Staggering, she shook her head no. It was in the nightstand drawer in her room.

"Oh, God!" Unsure of what to do, Terry whirled around in search of some help. When Princess' knees buckled, nearly sending her to the ground, adrenaline shot through Terry's body as he caught her. He picked her up in his arms like she was a baby and took off running.

Their brief trip was bumpy as glimpses of the campus and students swept by. "You're gonna be alright." Terry was breathing hard and his sweat suit clung to his body. Persistently he chanted, "You're gonna be alright. You're gonna be alright." He passed Founder's Hall and ran through the lawn toward the dining hall and up past the academic buildings. "We're almost there," he said. "Hold on." Near Lincoln Hall somebody was calling her name, but she couldn't respond.

Terry burst through the doors of the infirmary. "Help her somebody! Help her, please! She's having an asthma attack!" A nurse standing nearby assisted Terry and placed Princess in a comfortable chair, putting a nebulizing mask over her nose and mouth, enabling her to breathe more easily. The nurse then held her right arm, taking her blood pressure and then her pulse.

Princess took in long, deep breaths. *Thank you, God! What a blessing it is to be able to breathe. Thank you, Terry!* Those were the last thoughts she remembered.

PRINCESS WAS disoriented as she awakened in the bland infirmary, wondering where she was. She looked around her unfamiliar surroundings and thought she was alone. Then she heard a phone ringing outside the door and scattered voices in the distance.

"Let's move her over here," said a soft, calm female voice. Princess caught a whiff of the nurse's perfume as the bed began to move. "Hey, there. How ya feeling?" Princess indicated her improvement by a simple wave of her hand. "Had a little excitement, huh?"

Princess replied affirmatively, this time with a slight nod. She was still lethargic and felt very woozy.

"Yes, but you're gonna be fine."

The nurse moved Princess to a private room and left her there for observation. As she drifted in and out of sleep, her disjointed mind replayed past memories: an old childhood friend they called String Bean played tag with her and could never catch her; the oatmeal her grandmother used to feed her; a speech that she gave when she was awarded the Golden Borough President award; how difficult it was to ride the bumper cars at Coney Island when she was four years old and her aunt had to rescue her out of a traffic jam.

Suddenly she recalled the terror in Terry's eyes, the fear in his voice, and the trembling of his body when he was carrying her to the infirmary. Princess was scared, too, but she was familiar with asthma attacks, and he probably wasn't. Doctors had said she would eventually grow out of it, and they were probably right. Only it hadn't happened yet.

PRINCESS CLUTCHED her book bag and straightened her shoulders as she approached Boravia's Administrative Building, to which she had been summoned.

"May I help you?" asked the dean's secretary, a gaunt white woman with muddy eyes and red frizzy hair.

"I was told to report to Mrs. Weinger today at 3:00."

"Yes, and whom shall I say—"

"There you are," Mrs. DeMarco said, appearing suddenly. "I'll take her in," she told the secretary, and escorted Princess down the corridor.

With its traditional mahogany furnishings, rich navy carpeting, and accessories in muted shades of blue, the beautifully designed office resembled a presidential suite.

A brown-haired white woman, smartly dressed in a gray suit, stood up from her desk chair.

"Mrs. Weinger, Dean of Students," she introduced herself as. "It's a pleasure to meet you, Princess. Please, sit down."

"Glad to meet you, Mrs. Weinger." Princess was nervous.

"I know you're wondering why we asked you to come here today."

"Yes."

"As you know, the tragic ordeal with Lisa Capote came as a shock to all of us," Mrs. Weinger began, clasping her hands together. "Authorities were baffled until you came forward with information about Lisa's Internet dating . . . if you want to call it that. At any rate, the police informed us just yesterday that the man who attacked Lisa turned out to be a 42-year-old man."

"What?"

"He was arrested over a week ago. He has a prior history of abducting teenage girls. Now, with the information you provided, the police questioned Lisa from a different perspective. She admitted to being ELCEE and that she had indeed planned to meet someone at the movies that day. The computer crime lab was unable to trace his e-mail, so the police obtained a warrant to narrow e-mail sites within a square-mile radius. Follow me?"

"Yes."

"Out of five convicted felons living in that area, police were able to get a positive I.D. from witnesses who attended a line-up. They also found a relatively new bruise and tested his DNA. The skin particles found underneath Lisa's nails were a dead-on match.Princess pressed her hand to her chest, staring beyond Mrs. Weinger in disbelief.

"So it seems that her so-called 'soul mate' fooled his way into her heart. And that wasn't all. He has a history of statutory rape with several girls, and was convicted twice."

"What!" Princess gasped.

"They're now suspecting that there might be a connection with the abducted girl who was found in the woods some months back. One woman, who witnessed the scene, said he was trying to put Lisa in the trunk of his car, but she had fought hard, and when she screamed, he jumped in the car and drove away."

Princess looked over at Mrs. DeMarco, who was listening as intently as she was.

"They'd planned to get together while she was out on a weekend pass," Mrs. Weinger continued. "According to Lisa they were supposed to meet precisely at a certain time by

Seidelman's Candle Shop. Once her friends were seated in the movie theatre Lisa saved an empty seat next to hers and used her shopping bags as an excuse to go to the car, but she was really going to find him. They had arranged that after they'd met, he would follow her back to the theatre and watch the movie with her. It certainly would've been a different kind of first date."

"But how did he know what she looked like?"

"Lisa said they downloaded pictures of themselves, but of course the picture she received was one of an attractive eighteen-year-old young man."

"Did she ever suspect that her attacker might be her soul-mate?" Princess asked. "Wasn't it all too much of a coincidence?"

"Well, obviously not to Lisa. She was supposed to meet him in an entirely different location from where she was attacked. She knew what he looked like, or so she thought. In her mind it was just an unfortunate act and she didn't connect the dots, so why even speak about it? Not to mention that meeting someone outside of school on a weekend pass is against school rules."

Princess grunted incredulously, glancing from one woman to the other.

"Had it not been for your special attention to detail, their relationship may have continued, and then, who knows . . . More importantly, though, this sends off a signal to us to caution our students against Internet intermingling. It's dangerous." Mrs. Weinger stood up and walked in front of her desk.

"Hard to believe this," Princess murmured softly.

"Well, it's true . . . and because of you, someone else will be spared."

Princess felt strangely victorious that she might have helped resolve a matter that had her school and the larger community on edge. A simple follow-up on an instinct and getting the information into the right hands may have changed the course of another human being's fate. All of her other petty concerns suddenly shrunk in size.

"How is Lisa doing?" Princess asked.

"She's doing well. She's more shocked than anything. Her parents will keep her home as long as they need to. Now," she said, leaning back on her desk, "there was another reason we called you here today. Mr. Capote, Lisa's father, is an alumnus of Boravia and wanted to express his gratitude to you."

"To me?"

"He chairs The International Tour Committee, which sponsors the Paris Tour each year for the junior-senior French Club. I understand you're doing exceptionally well learning the language . . . so it looks like they're going to make an exception next year and include a sophomore."

Princess looked confused.

"Next year, you will be a part of that tour."

Princess turned first to Mrs. Weinger and then to Mrs. DeMarco. "Did you say Paris? As in France?"

The women laughed, easing the tension in the room.

"Yes," confirmed Mrs. DeMarco, taking hold of her hand. "You're going on a trip to France, sweetie . . . and you deserve it."

"Congratulations!" Mrs. Weinger hailed. "Paris is a beautiful city."

"My God . . . I don't know what to say."

"Nothing more to say. We're grateful."

"And so am . . . thank you."

"No, we thank you."

Well, now, folks in Telham Park are gonna flip when they hear this.

EMILY CONSATTI passed Princess her newspaper in history class as they watched *Secrets of the Ancient World*. A faint shock rushed through her as she read the ominous headline in the *Boravia Times* that read:

TEENAGE GIRLS ABDUCTED FOR BLACK MARKET PROSTITUTION

The harsh realities regarding what was really going on behind the tragedy horrified Princess as the details unfolded. She learned that Lisa Capote's attacker wasn't working alone and was part of a bigger racket to use young girls. By the end of the school day it seemed as if the whole school had read the article; it was the talk on campus. Princess rushed to the library and e-mailed the details to Nadira and called her family to inform them of the news.

THERE WERE great concert performances and then there was the magic of Zulek, the gifted Russian pianist.

The round-faced, curly-headed child prodigy was in his senior year at Boravia and had already played more than 200 concerts in ten different countries. His dynamic performance after school left them all feeling happy—which is what he calls the philosophy behind his music—but more important than being transported into a good mood, they were inspired.

Later that evening, Princess settled into her new-found sanctuary—a private study room on the third floor of the library. It was an escape that allowed her some alone time to listen to music and work on the 'Small Talk' column uninterrupted. Also pressing on her agenda was to finish reading James Baldwin's *Go Tell It on the Mountain*, the novel she'd chosen to read and critique for English class.

They called us Negroes back in those days. Huh! Insulting then, but now we choose to use the word.

Princess fell back in laughter at Roy's dialogue, the main character of the book, and that's when she caught Terry's eyes. He was standing at the door making a peace sign.

"Hey, girl, ya busy?" he asked, entering the small room. "A peace offering. Here." He placed a small package in front of her.

The angelic sound of dangling chimes brought a smile to her face. "Aww, it's beautiful. Thank you."

"Like you," he said, grabbing a chair. "How you feelin'?"

"I'm good."

"Can I sit here?"

"Sure. Oh, this is so cute."

"A little souvenir from Boston. We won the game."

"Good for you." Princess was cool and poised as she dangled the chimes, delighting in the percussive, heavenly sound.

"We need to . . . I need to talk." Terry's shaken words matched the pinched, serious look on his face.

Amused by his trepidation, Princess showed no reaction.

"C'mon, we ain't no strangers. I feel bad enough that I caused you to have an asthma attack. You scared me to death, girl." Terry moved his chair closer to her. "But why did you turn on me like that?"

Princess' gaze fell on the dangling chimes again and while appreciating their beauty, her expression suddenly changed. "What do I look like to you?"

"I don't . . . what do you mean?"

"What do I look like to you?"

Befuddled, he paused to think about a response. One he thought she'd want to hear. "You look like a Princess to me."

"Then I should be treated like one."

"As far as I know, you—"

"So Sherita was right?"

"Sherita?" His face grew serious now, almost to a scowl. "Right about what?"

"Your girlfriend, Corvette?"

"Who's . . . I only know one person by that name and she lives in the Palisades."

"Yeah, *that* Corvette," she stressed, shifting the chimes. They rang even louder. "You had the audacity to invite her here."

He backed away and stared awkwardly. "Wait a minute. I'm not—"

"What did you think?" Princess asked, cutting him off. "We were gonna jump rope together or you were gonna be holding me with one hand, her with another?"

"Okay, you lost me," he stammered.

"Here I was thinkin' you and I were kickin' it, and then Sherita introduces me to your girlfriend. She was telling me the truth all the time, but you denied it."

"You buggin'!" he argued. "That's not my girlfriend. I know her from home and—"

"You lied!" exclaimed Princess, ignoring his denials. "And you thought you could get away with it."

"Lied about what? Okay, wait. I'm missing something here. You're telling me I'm with some girl that I hardly even know?"

"Oh, now you're trying to say you don't know her?"

"I'm sayin,' I don't know her like *that*."

"Sherita introduced her to me as your friend that *you* invited here, and Corvette didn't object."

"And you believed her?" Terry chuckled. "You don't know her."

"I know enough to know that between your lies and hers, y'all deserve each other."

"Ay, don't go there on me like that. Look, if I invited Corvette here, why wasn't I with her? I saw her, said what's up and kept it movin'. I didn't know why she was here. I figured she came up to see Sherita. They were hanging around the locker room at halftime and I never saw her again."

"I don't know if you spent time with her or not. After Sherita introduced her to me, I left."

"And after the game I was looking for you."

"I'm supposed to believe that?"

"That's right . . .'cause that's the way it was."

The momentary silence allowed them both to take a deep breath. "So that's what's been up with you," Terry realized, sliding his hand from his forehead to the back of his neck as he began to understand Princess' behavior. "We need to talk . . . I mean really talk."

"I'm listening."

"It's a long, long story." Terry stood up and paced around the small space.

How's he gonna talk his way out of this? Look at him. I almost feel sorry for him. But wait a minute; I'm the victim here. I'm the one who got jammed, made a fool of. Huh! He'll have to come up with something miraculous for me to ever trust him again.

"Can I talk to you tomorrow?"

"No, today. Whatever's on your mind, *now* is the time." Princess shook the chimes again and Terry's tall frame slid down into the chair.

"I'm gonna tell you something. This is on the serious low-low . . . between us, okay?"

Princess eased back and stared intently.

"Sherita and me . . ." he began solemnly. "We go back."

Uh oh. Do I really want to hear this?

"Two summers ago I was going out with this girl named Nikki, from around the way. Me and her was mad cool. Now

I knew Sherita . . . since she was a iddy biddy thing. She was like the cute little girl that had a crush on the older boy when you was growin' up, know what I'm sayin'?"

"Uh huh."

"I would tease her sometimes, make her laugh and stuff. But then she grew up and started hanging out. She had a little sumpthin' sumpthin' going on, you know a lot of dudes was on her. Now me and Nikki was tight. Everybody knew it. So Sherita's mom and my uncle went to school together, and they're still good friends. She would come over to my uncle's for barbecues or drinks sometimes and would always bring Sherita. I knew she had a little thing for me, but she also knew Nikki was my girl."

Princess grunted as she fixed her eyes on his.

"But she was persistent, determined, you know . . . just threw herself at me."

"What!" Princess felt as if she'd been hit in the face with ice-cold water.

"I didn't ask for it. And it only happened one time."

"But you didn't refuse her, either!" Princess railed, a stream of anger shooting through her.

"Well, what was I supposed to do?" he shrugged. "How many dudes you know gonna say no?"

"A decent one would." Her voice was sterile and she refused to allow her face to register the extent of her disappointment. Turning away from him, she took a deep breath and sighed heavily. *My instincts warned me from the beginning, but I guess I was in denial. It's out now and it's true. Sherita and Terry . . . I feel like I'm gonna puke.*

Princess turned back toward him and saw the shame resting in his eyes. "But that wasn't all of it."

"There's more?" Princess dropped the chimes deliberately and cast a scathing glance at him.

"Look, I'm not proud of this, but at least I'm telling you the truth."

"You wanna medal? For doing what you're supposed to do? After I've been played like a twelve-string guitar? You must be smokin'—"

"Nobody played you, just lemme finish . . . please?" He reached for her hand but she snatched it back and turned away.

"Come on, don't treat me like this," he pleaded. "I'm being straight with you."

"Just . . . go on." She turned back to him with a look of sheer disgust.

"Okay. So out of the clear blue one day she comes up to me, right? Nikki was standing no more than six feet in front of us talking to one of her girls. That's when Sherita told me she was pregnant."

No amount of theatrics in the world could have camouflaged Princess' astonishment. As she sank back into her chair, withdrawing further from Terry's rueful eyes, her heart sank into her stomach.

Terry cupped his hand around Princess' fist. "Listen, listen, she wanted me to break up with Nikki and be with her 'cause she was pregnant. I told her no. She said she was gonna have the baby and Nikki was gonna find out anyway, so I might as well let her go now. I was caught out there and had no choice. I figured I could back off Nikki for a minute and that would give me a chance to try to convince Sherita not to have the baby."

"What was she, thirteen?" Princess asked.

"She had just turned fourteen, so you know I was . . . and that's the summer I found out I got the scholarship to come here. So I told Nikki some story about how I didn't want any commitments 'cause I was leaving and how I wanted to be friends, you know, see other people. Nikki wasn't havin' it. 'Cause she was fine and there was ten other dudes waiting in line to be with her, exclusively. She was too mature for all that cheatin' madness. So she walked. I felt so bad 'cause I know she was really hurt."

Princess couldn't get a clear reading on his sincerity because all she could see was a vision of a little Terry running around.

"Anyway, my scholarship and *everything* was on the line. My moms would've went ballistic, and I told you about her blood pressure. That would have killed her—and me, too! So I told my uncle, and he said he was gonna get with her moms and arrange for all of us to talk. When I told Sherita what we were going to do, she got scared and claimed she lost the baby."

"What?" Princess asked, astonished. "Did she really lose it?"

"Heck no! There was no baby from the start. She couldn't give me one detail on how she lost the baby, no test results, never went to a doctor or anything. She was lying from the start, but the damage was already done."

"Oh, my God!" Princess leaned forward, and in a strange way felt relieved.

"It was too late to go back with Nikki, so I had to leave it alone. Sherita ruined everything." Terry fell back like he had just released a thousand-pound burden. "I'm telling you what she did," he continued, sitting up straight. "Okay, so I'm done with her, cool. Then she went and applied to this school . . . and got accepted! You know what I felt like when I saw her moving onto this campus? No, you don't know," he said, falling back again. "If this scholarship wasn't so important to me I would have left. So she knows I don't have anything for her, so she just tries to make trouble for anybody I'm with."

Terry paused for a minute with a questioning look on his face. "Come to think of it, I never knew Sherita and Corvette to be friends . . . not like that. Corvette used to go out with one of my boys."

"Well, maybe they were brought together by you."

"Princess, you don't believe that, I know. C'mon, this is so transparent. She wanted you to think that, but I'm telling you what it is." Terry was adamant in his position. "I can prove it, too."

"So what am I supposed to do?" Princess asked. "Pretend this didn't happen? Be with you now? And look like a fool in front of all the people who know?"

"Like who? Nobody knows Corvette or who she is or why she was here. I didn't even know . . . and I really don't give a rip about what people think."

"You're not the one looking stupid, either."

"And neither are you. Think I'd put you in a position like that? Sherita has nothing to do with me and you."

"She doesn't think so . . . and I'm not gonna have her stalking me." Princess paused, momentarily reflecting on Sherita's deceitfulness. *I'll introduce her to the Brooklyn side of me, and it won't be pretty. So you better tame her if you know what I know before things gets ugly.*

"I didn't come to Boravia to get involved in some soap opera nonsense, and I'm not about to fight over you."

"It's not like that," Terry objected. "I'm not expecting you—"

"Where I come from it's not a privilege to have a guy. 'Cause just like yourself, dogs will get busy with any female who wags her tail."

"Now how you gonna—"

"You had a girlfriend and you let Sherita come between y'all?" Princess broke in. "So what you're telling me is, if I was your girl you would allow her to come between us. No, thank you!"

"I would never mess with her, ever again! So that wouldn't even be an issue."

Princess stood up abruptly and gathered her books. "Why didn't you tell me this before . . . when I asked you to be straight-up with me?" Blasted expectations dashed her future hopes and the feeling that she had been betrayed overwhelmed her. "I'm out of here."

Terry snatched the chimes she'd left on the table and blocked the door. "Can't we be friends and start all over again? Don't let her get away with this."

Princess looked into his pitiful eyes, and tried hard not to surrender to his suffering.

"See, this is exactly what she wants. Kill all our plans—"

"What plans?"

"I thought you were gonna be my ridin' partner. Look how well you're doin' now. And what about The Social next week, you're telling me it's all squashed now?" He placed the chimes inside her backpack. "I'm sorry . . . for real."

"I'm sorry, too. You know, if you were a different person maybe I could overlook this, but I think you think you can have your way with girls, anytime you want, but I'm not one of them."

"Where did you get that from? I never thought about you like that."

Silence inched between them. Princess needed time to digest it all. "I'll think about it," she said, moving out of the room.

"Let me walk you back to Bryant."

"No, no, I'm good. I'll see you later."

"You're gonna call me?"

Princess waved briefly behind her back and made a quick departure.

twelve

"Was that lightning?" asked Princess, catching what looked like a flash in the sky. The girls in Suite 210 barely noticed the light or the crackling thunder that followed as they frenetically prepared for the Millennium Social.

"I think it was," replied Saba, taking a sip of her cosmopolitan. Bottles of vodka had had been smuggled into dorm rooms through Boravia's underground, and with a mixture of raspberry liqueur, cranberry juice and a twist of lemon, all was good in Saba's world. In the mirror she approved her long, luscious eyelashes that completed her eye-makeup, thanks to the magic of a brush wand and several coats of black mascara. Preferring a tanned look, she used a bronzer that gave her skin that flawless, healthy glow. And the pink-shimmered, plum-tinged lip gloss was a perfect match. *Mwah!*

Slipping into her dress for the second time—this time with a pair of thongs on— Tyler uttered, "Much better."

Stephanie examined her profile in the full-length mirror and began gyrated her hips in admiration. "Uh-oh, check it out, y'all. Work it, work it, work that thang," she conducted to the beat of the music, radiant in her deep-purple velvet dress and gold accessories, spinning around to test the look.

Sherita had been dressed and out of the door before all of them.

"It smells good in here," said Snoopy, coming out of the shower as lightening struck again. "Whoa . . . did you see that?"

"Looks like a storm," said Tyler looking out of the window through the blinds. Torrential rain had driven temperatures well above normal and big drops of water pelted hard against the windows, which should have been a consideration for heavier clothing for the night. But it wasn't. It would take more than bad weather conditions to dampen the spirit of Boravians. They were charged and feverishly eager to attend the most anticipated event of the year—storm or no storm.

"Don't forget your camera," Princess reminded Stephanie as they headed down to the lobby. It was crowded with gorgeous girls whispering eagerly to each other, smiling, perfumed and glamorous.

"They'll be here in about three minutes," Stephanie said, closing the call on her cell phone.

As a special bonus for an undefeated season thus far, Coach Myerson had promised the team their own private transportation to escort their dates to the affair in.

"Oh, my God!" Princess shrieked, watching the black sleek stretch limousine pull up. "We're only going to—"

"That's how the rich folks do it," Stephanie grinned. "I told you what they were planning do 'cause I overheard them talking about it. It's supposed to be a surprise, so act like it is."

Terry and Damien stepped out of the darkened back seat like professional athletes, shielded by the driver's super-sized umbrella.

"There go my baby!" beamed Stephanie.

Princess looked at them in wide-eyed amazement. "OH MY GOD!"

"If I don't make it in tonight, you will understand," teased Stephanie

"It's too slippery out there for the spider woman act." Princess laughed but then said seriously, "Don't even think about it."

Like a Hollywood premiere, the "who's with who" and "who's wearing what" radar was on full alert capturing radical *avant-garde* and *super-chic* fashions alongside dapper tuxedos. The couples stepped out of the luxury limousine, then up the stairs under a shimmering gold canopy and a red-carpeted floor. At the platform, and by design, photographers were ready as the couples posed proudly for pictures.

Founder's Hall had been transformed into a veritable ballroom with crystal stars twinkling beneath a velvet-blue simulated sky. The elegant ambiance engaged all of their senses, from the scented candles to the dramatic yet simple flowers. It had all the trappings of opulent loveliness in its purple and gold decorum.

Terry looked amazingly handsome under the dim lights. So good, in fact, Princess was able to blot out her bad lingering feelings about him and enjoy the evening. And that's what Boravians did, over three hundred of them.

The music dictated their movements on the mirror-waxed floors, altering from easy rap to the latest energy-zapping pop. Kim Taylor's "I Dream a Night" slowed the pace, allowing the students to socialize and sip refreshments.

Princess and Terry were flowing to the lyrics of the song, doing an easy two-step and talking until they found themselves practically alone and on display.

"That tux is working on you," Princess said, leading them off the dance floor.

"I can do a little something when I have to" he said, looking down at himself. Then he waved one arm and partially bowed. "And you, my Princess, are the envy of all who stand before us this evening."

Princess was blushing. "You're crazy . . . I'm convinced."

"Nah, but seriously, you're beautiful." Wearing her hair swooped up in a bush of kinky curls, simple makeup and in her form-fitting ice-blue gown, Terry was dazzled.

Meandering through the crowd, he inched up close to her and whispered, "The way I seez it, weez 'bout de bestest lookin' twosome he-uh."

Princess laughed heartily and his rendition of a southern accent. "Oh, and speaking of twosome, how were you able to get me a riding habit?" she asked squeezing his hand.

"Just did."

"I was shocked when I unzipped the suit bag and saw the outfit. Then you sent me the helmet and the boots. I was ready to jump on Satin right then and there. And how much did all that cost? I don't want you spending—"

"Did everything fit?"

"Sure did. And how did you know what—"

"That's all that matters," he said, looking around proudly. "I have a little influence 'round these parts, so don't you worry 'bout that."

They held on closely to each other as they socialized, posed for photographs and wandered around the room, commenting on its splendor.

"You hungry?"

"Ahhh—"

"A little bit?"

"I don't know. It's kinda hard for me to be hungry at a time like this."

"Maybe this'll wake up your taste buds," said Terry leading her to the buffet of succulent appetizers. The exquisite display of food—succulent fruit, the delicate canapés, smoked salmon, finely cut roast beef, and savory meatball-and-cherry tomato shish kabobs—surrounding the four-foot ice sculpture was sinfully abundant.

"Now this is my kinda living," Damien said, approaching them, enjoying a beef kabob. Stephanie was with him, savoring a plate of shrimp and pasta from the seafood tower. "Did the mystery man show up yet?" Stephanie whispered.

"That's who's missing," said Terry. "The wicked witch of the West."

"Who, your girl?" Princess teased, giving him a slight elbow.

Stephanie snickered and rolled her eyes. "She probably wants to make a grand entrance with her secret admirer."

"Whoever he is, I feel for him," Damien mumbled.

"Who's the po' sucka anyway?" asked Christopher.

"We don't actually know," said Stephanie, passing a questioning look among the girls. "And she doesn't, either. He never told her who he was, but he did say he would pick her up tonight."

When the music switched gears, they returned to the dance floor. Terry threw himself into the rhythm. He was as good a dancer as he was an athlete. She raised her hands up in the air and Terry met them with his, their eyes locked in understanding. He didn't exactly make her 'heart-throb' list any more—he was now more like a good friend, or a big brother, perhaps. Actually, she hadn't decided where Terry would fit in her world. And right now, it wasn't important. After all the hard work and stress of making it at Boravia, she was finally having some fun.

꜍ ꜍ ꜍

Sherita couldn't resist primping as she admired herself over and over again in the lobby mirror at Bryant Hall while waiting for her mystery date. Her fiery-red Lycra dress fit her snug and tight. Glancing at herself from all angles, she approved of the deep V-cut that exposed her back and the gold satin sandals that matched her purse. Though the night was still young, she agonized over every moment that passed.

"Maybe you should go on," Mrs. Hinckly advised. She'd been watching Sherita pace up and down for nearly an hour. "He might already be there."

"Without me?" Sherita retorted, insinuating the stupidity of the statement.

"You never know, something may have happened."

"And how am I supposed to know who he is?"

"You have an idea, don't you?"

The thought of Blair waiting for her brought on a smile. "Well, sure."

Any thoughts she may have had of leaving were canceled as the downpour intensified, turning the darkness into a light gray sheet of rain.

After another twenty minutes passed and the rain had let up a bit, her impatience got the better of her. She couldn't wait another minute. Hastily, she grabbed her umbrella and shot out the door to Founder's Hall.

꜍ ꜍ ꜍

Following a blitz of club and rap hits, The DJ slowed his pace. Couples retreated to their groups while they enjoyed second and third helpings of the delicious appetizers.

"Don't you think Langsford dances funny?" asked Snoopy, watching his every move. Snoopy had transformed into an elegant young woman in her asymmetrical burgundy-violet two-piece ensemble, even while depositing whole meatballs and chicken fingers into her mouth. .

"I don't know," replied Princess. I wasn't looking at how he's dancing, but in that tuxedo, his whole look is polished."

"Looks even whiter in that black, don't you think? And I've never seen him do that wet look thing to his hair."

"I think it looks good!"

"Um . . . guess so," she muttered. "But I'm havin' a problem with him dancing, kinda off-beat with that rhythm of his. It's like he's moving a notch or two faster and never catches the beat."

"Well, slow him down," Princess suggested, admiring Malira's stunning gown.

"And how am I supposed to teach a white boy how to dance?" Snoopy put her hand to her mouth, realizing the ears that were all around her. In a lower voice she said, "You know they're allergic to rhythm."

"Stop being so critical," Princess advised. "Some of them out there are dancing pretty well."

"Well he's not one of them. Let's get some more chicken and shrimp," Snoopy said, gauging Langsford's whereabouts.

"Are you hungry or what, Snoopy?"

"Well . . . I only ate once today, and with all the running around I had to do, I burned it all off. And you know I don't want to stuff my face in front of Langsford. So stand here with me while I get full."

Terry, Damien and some other Boravian boys had parted from their dates to eat as well.

"So the next time we dance just watch him, okay?" asked Snoopy.

"How am I supposed to watch him when I'm doing my own thing?" Princess protested, selecting grapes and strawberries from the fruit platter.

"You know how to do it. You can turn and glance at him, turn back to me and throw me a sign on the DL and tell me how bad it is."

"If he's moving too fast, just guide him into the rhythm," Princess said.

"How do I do that?"

"You never taught anybody how to dance?"

"Not really."

Flashbacks of Snoopy's dancing came before her. "Uh oh, I forgot," she hastened quickly. "Never mind."

"Now how you gonna talk about me like that, Princess?"

"I'm not talking about you, Boo. You know you my baby girl and everything. But we both know you could use a little assistance when it comes to dancin'."

"Okay, maybe a little," Snoopy admitted. "But I'm still doing better than he is. You know, something's telling me to ask him if he thinks he can dance."

"Ask him? How you gonna ask somebody if they *think* they can dance?"

"It's a fair question."

"And what do you expect him to say, no? Everybody thinks they can dance, even when they can't. That's like asking someone if they think they look good."

Saba and Stephanie stepped in their circle. Saba's clothes were indicative of her personality—sassy and stylish. She looked terrific in an all-black ensemble—a high-cut wool jersey tank top with a long, wool crepe skirt. Punctuating her look was her lengthy black hair that hung loosely down the sides of her face. For the occasion, she had the bottom half of her hair streaked in blonde.

"Okay, this music is putting me to sleep," said Stephanie. "I'm ready to get this party started again."

"Chill, wild girl," said Princess. "I know you 'bout ready to pop out of that dress and everything, but give it a minute. People are still coming in."

"Where's Sherita and her hot piece of property that's been smoozing her?" Saba asked.

"Doesn't look like she got here yet. At least I don't see her," replied Stephanie, scanning the room. "I can't wait to see who he is."

"That makes all of us," said Snoopy.

With her digital camera, Tyler caught them in a natural pose as she arrived from the left side of the room. Her look was one of simple elegance: a gold, conventionally tailored, haltered gown, slit up to the knee. As she moved in closer, they all graciously posed.

"Members of the best suite at Bryant say 'Cheerio' to the mates in London," said Stephanie.

"Cheerio," they hailed in unison.

⧫ ⧫ ⧫

Sherita's damp feet turned cold, and she was now regretting the long dash she made from Bryant Hall with only a small umbrella and a wool shawl to protect her. Blair had not arrived at Founder's Hall yet, as she learned from several student ushers. Mrs. Hinckly was on alert and knew how to reach her in the event he showed up at the dorm. Impatiently, she waited inside a small, recessed area of the lobby where no one could see her yet she had a clear view of everyone coming and going.

What is taking this man so long? Sherita tested her perfume on her inner wrist, now struggling to smell it with quick, deep inhalations. For two days she'd prepared for this evening and it was steadily slipping away. Shivering, she could hear loud cheers of celebration and smelled the tantalizing aroma of the food, tormenting her taste buds. Her breath mints had fizzled to little pebble-sized balls and she fished in her bag to find some more.

"Sherita Lawson, is that you?" asked a student usher.

"Yes, that's me," she replied, her face brightening. "Yes, that's me."

"There's a phone call for you."

She rushed out to the small office down the corridor filled with anticipation. "Hello?"

"Hello, Sherita. This is Mrs. Hinckley."

"Yes, what is it?"

"Someone just delivered a package for you."

"What's in it?"

"I don't know. It's beautifully wrapped in a gift box with a big bow around it."

"Well, who delivered it? Is he waiting?"

"No one is here. Whoever it was rang the bell and dashed off."

"I'm coming back to get it." Sherita hung up the phone fast, reacting without thinking and made her way to the door.

Halfway to Bryant Hall, the heavy downpour returned. It was cold and damp and her dress was getting wet. Moving swiftly, she inadvertently stepped into a huge puddle of water and got one of her sandals soaked. Still, she pressed on. This evening would be a success. She was determined to see to it.

≈ ≈ ≈

"Alright girls, you're looking good out there," the smooth-sounding DJ's voice bellowed over the PA system. He was a young white man, tall and handsome, with a rhythm like Elvis. "We're gonna reverse roles here for a minute and the girls are gonna grab a partner. Wait a minute!" He held up his index finger and the music paused. "But it has to be a partner other than your date."

Hard applause and whistles of approval exploded throughout the room and the music resumed. The boys stood coolly, awaiting their invitations. Startled by the flipped script, the girls looked around uneasily.

"Decisions, decisions. No time for contemplating," the DJ called out. "Just do it!"

Princess went straight to Langsford and grabbed his hand. Tyler, Saba, and Stephanie followed Princess' lead, grabbing each other's dates, and Snoopy ended up paired with Terry.

Langsford had a small head and thin, narrow features on his tall, slender frame. The music triggered some emotional excitement in him, and a gleam burned in his eyes when he moved. Princess carefully took charge and led the rhythm. Bouncing in sync with the music, she took his hand when he moved too fast, and gradually slowed down, conducting the timing. It wasn't long before Langsford and Princess were dancing at an even pace. Enjoying it, they remained on the floor through three R&B hits.

"That was awesome," Langsford said, as they parted. "You're a great dancer."

"So are you, dude. Let's do it again sometime."

Terry and Princess found each other for the slow dance. She felt so comforted in his embrace and he swayed with her so naturally.

"Oh, she is beautiful," said one of the girls, as the crowd began applauding.

"Who is she?" another girl asked.

"Is that her father? Oh, my God!" exclaimed an unfamiliar voice.

"That's Lisa," said Tyler, hovering next to Princess.

"Lisa who?"

"Capote. Looks like she's with her father."

Lisa Capote was a petite girl with a round face, thick eyebrows and long brown hair. Terry and Princess joined in the applause as Lisa and her father moved to the center of the floor. She walked proudly in her silk and chiffon sequined gown alongside her distinguished father, who wore formal military attire. When Mr. Capote embraced his daughter, she began to cry. In the emotionally charged moment, many of the girls began to tear up as well, including Princess.

"Ladies and Gentleman, Mr. and Ms. Capote," announced Headmaster Delmore.

Everyone applauded generously as she and her father danced to a cool, R & B song by Charisse.

≈ ≈ ≈

Sherita tore into the gift box, throwing the ribbon to the floor. Inside was a beautiful, white double-rose corsage sprinkled with gold glitter. She snatched it out, slipped her hand through the wristlet, and that's when she found the insides of her hands smeared in black ink.

"Oh no, my God! What is this?" She removed the corsage, staining her hands even more and threw it to the floor. "It's not coming off!" she cried, rubbing her hands together. It seemed like something out of a bad dream.

Mrs. Hinckly rose up in wild-eyed astonishment from the desk. "What in the world? Try to get it off with soap."

"This can't be happening!" Sherita cried, running toward the restroom. "It can't be." Her forty-dollar manicure was ruined, and the hour was becoming critically late.

Mrs. Hinckly picked up the corsage, examined the box and found a note in it. "Who sent this to you?" she asked when Sherita returned. Her hands and nails were still smeared in ink.

Sherita snatched the note, which read: Sincere apologies. I'm running late. Meet me at Founder's Hall. With all the tension and commotion, Sherita's heart instantly felt lighter. There had to be some explanation for the ink, she reasoned. Right now there was a date awaiting her, and nothing was going to stop her. She dashed frantically out the door once again.

"Sherita! Mrs. Hinckly called, trailing behind her. "Where are you going, child? You've got ink all over you and it's pouring out there!"

The relentless rain altered the direction of its rage as Sherita sloshed through puddles of water, trying to make it back to Founder's Hall. The whirling winds were pulling her umbrella outward exposing her curly hair weave that was quickly going limp. As she swerved around trying to get the umbrella to snap forward in place, she accidentally slipped off the curb, breaking the heel of her shoe.

"No!" she screamed, rising on the ball of her wet foot. Balancing herself on the other foot she tried to detach the heel completely, but the nails were too stubborn. Bouncing forward, Sherita's umbrella could no longer handle the pressure of the wind and she fought and struggled with it until she finally threw it away. Her shawl was all that was left to use to shield her from becoming totally drenched. She raised it over her head and continued moving.

Counting her steps through the driving rain, she could see Founder's Hall appearing closer and closer and the black limousine that had pulled up in front of it, too. Sherita stopped cold when she saw Blair stepping out of the luxurious automobile and reaching back into the car.

"Blair!" she yelled excitedly.

Suddenly Zorley, a popular junior, appeared by his side, who—by any standards—was gorgeous. Her bugle-beaded, silver strapless dress was gracefully adorned with a muted silver silk wrap. The gown's slight train made it appear as if she were floating when she walked. Sherita went numb watching Blair and Zorley proudly posing for pictures. As if in a nightmare, she wanted to run away from the scene in the hopes that she would wake up and find it all was a bad dream.

The tears fell freely as she made her way through the soggy, wet grounds back to Bryant Hall. Rewinding the events of the evening and realizing that her mystery date hadn't turned out to be Blair or anyone, for that matter, she wept loudly. Her body shivered with cold as the clammy rain penetrated her thin dress.

"Young lady, hello," a woman said, "Can I help you?"

She walked along the edges of the curb, so absorbed in bemoaning her misery she didn't see or hear the car approaching.

"Young lady, excuse me," the woman persisted. "Sherita, is that you?" It was Ms. Morgan.

In a daze, Sherita barely nodded.

"What are you doing out here?" Ms. Morgan asked and flung open the passenger door. "It's freezing out there. Get in!"

Inside the car Sherita said nothing, ignoring Mrs. Morgan's questions. "Look at your clothes. And your hair . . . and where's your coat? What happened?"

Sherita cried silently and stared obliviously into the stormy darkness, trembling from the wetness that had seeped into her skin.

❋ ❋ ❋

Following the formal sit-down dinner, the night moved into high gear. Right before dessert, the contests began. Princess couldn't believe they had formed a "Soul Train" line. Each couple anxiously awaited their chance in the spotlight. The feeling no longer was one of a "formal" affair, and the partygoers just went for it, flips, splits, cartwheels and all. Some of the white boys came out with some head-shaking, body slamming numbers that she didn't understand, but she applauded anyway.

Princess joined in the line with her foot-stomping, finger-popping Brooklyn grooves, and Terry followed closely behind. Stephanie came out with multiple spins, balancing herself on the balls of her feet. Then she shook her hips, gyrating to the floor in even rhythms, teasing the crowd. Moving back to back, she and Damien did a number in sync, taking it to the floor. The party then sailed into the electric slide, led by the staff, The students joined in laughingly to the old school favorite.

Following the wave of protracted "show off" energy, the DJ cruised into the mellow sounds of Mantara as unique desserts were served and the awards were presented. The "Best Dressed," "Most Popular," and "Most Accomplished" students were announced for each grade, with the freshman class called last. Kenneth and Suzanne were named Most Accomplished. David and Carol won Best Dressed. Stephanie and Damien won Best Dancers. And finally, the "Civic" award was about to be announced.

Stephanie was enjoying on a chocolate truffle and reached for Tyler's camera, preparing to take a shot.

"This award goes to the newest kid on the block," Headmaster Delmore began. "One who's made remarkable strides academically, shown civic interest, and brought innovation into our extracurricular activities. It is with great pride and pleasure that I present this award to . . . Princess Brixton."

Depositing a gold-dusted crepe into her mouth, Princess almost gagged as the applause sounded. In the surreal moment she thought for a second that there might be another person who shared her name.

"That's you!" Terry exclaimed, applauding.

Out of all the applause, Princess could hear the girls of Suite 210 shouting her name as Terry escorted her toward the stage.

"It's nice to meet you," greeted Lisa, as they embraced, her watery blue eyes glistening.

"Nice to meet you."

"A Princess and a savior. I'm honored to meet you," Lisa's father said, taking both her hands and offering her a loving embrace.

"So nice to meet you, Mr. Capote, and thank you. Paris—"

"My pleasure. A small token for what you did."

Princess received the plaque and was congratulated by every member of the school staff.

❧ ❧ ❧

"Sickaplayin' . . . whudthafrigin . . . youletanutha . . ." Sherita jammed both her shoes inside the second floor trash can, mumbling inaudible phrases under her breath.

"What are you doing?" asked Ms. Morgan, following her into Suite 210.

"I don't have any need for a shoe with a broken heel!" Then she pushed the suite door with such force that it banged loudly against the sidewall.

"That's a brand-new pair of shoes. The heel can be fixed."

"I don't need the memory," she lamented, snatching bobby pins out of her hair. She pulled at one piece so hard the weave-glue loosened, causing the track to slide out of position. So she dug into her scalp, pulled the track out completely, and flung it across the room. Frustrated that the whole evening had been a waste, she began pulling at all the tracks in her hair, ripping out some of her own in the process.

"I want to go home!" she said, standing abruptly, and made her way over to her locker.

"You can't leave now. It's after nine o'clock."

"I'll call my mother to come and get me." Sherita was so upset the combination of her lock escaped her. "This stupid thing won't open," she snapped, pulling at it. Then she took her fist to the locker door and banged on it repeatedly, as if she were punishing it.

"Wait!" Ms. Morgan insisted, forcing her to sit down. "Calm yourself and tell me what happened. What are those black marks on your hands?"

Sherita observed the stains, now absorbed into her skin. She rubbed her hands briskly, then pressed her thumb over the soiled areas, hoping to see a sign of their removal. Several of her acrylic nails had been ruined, too. Covering her face with her hands, she began wailing profusely.

"What happened tonight?" Ms. Morgan asked, sitting next to her. "I don't get it. You changed your mind and turned around?" she queried. "You and your date had an argument?"

When Sherita removed her hands, tears mixed with black mascara had streaked down her cheeks and darkened her eyelids, simulating two black eyes. The dazzling, dreamy-eyed, peach-skinned beauty had disappeared under smeared makeup.

"Stop crying, Sherita. I need to hear you. C'mon, tell me what happened." Ms. Morgan pulled out some loose tissues from her purse and allowed Sherita to purge her sorrow. "C'mon, wipe away those tears," she told her.

There was a lengthy moment of silence. So long that Ms. Morgan, who was wearing a black sequined dress with a crepe wool wrap, thought she might call someone else to attend to the matter while she joined the festivities.

"Did you have a fight with your date? Did he cancel out on you or what?" Ms. Morgan probed, making one last attempt to get her talking.

She shook her head, indicating a 'no.'

"So what . . . wait a minute. Did you have a date?"

Sherita blew her nose hard and regained her composure. "I went there to meet him," she said finally.

"Okay. What student is this?"

"I don't know."

Ms. Morgan stared at her, bewildered. "But . . . how . . . could . . . you . . . meet someone when you don't know who it is?"

"I *thought* I knew. You know the roses I'd been receiving?"

"Yes."

"They were coming from somewhere anonymously, but I thought he was playing a game."

"He who? What's the student's name?"

"It doesn't matter. In the note he said he'd pick me up tonight and we'd go together. So I waited. When he didn't show, I thought something may have happened, so I went to Founder's . . . thinking I could meet him there."

"But you didn't know who you were looking for."

"I told you, I was so sure I knew who he was and was expecting—"

"Oh . . . okay, I gotcha."

"Then Mrs. Hinckly called and said someone had left a gift box for me at the door. I ran all the way back to find a corsage and a note. It said he was still coming. When I put the corsage on, all this black ink smeared all over my hands."

"Hold on, back up a minute," Ms. Morgan said. "So you decided to go even when you realized how late it was. And?"

Sherita turned away and quickly mumbled the rest. "I tripped and broke my heel, my hair and clothes got all wet, and I just didn't want to go at that point."

"Why would somebody do something like this to you?"

Sherita didn't reply.

"But whoever it is will receive repercussions like—"

"No," Sherita interrupted curtly. "I don't want to get into it. This never happened."

"We don't tolerate these types of pranks here," Ms. Morgan asserted. "You missed a beautiful event that you and your parents made great preparations for—"

"I don't care about any of that. I just want to go home." Sherita squirmed out of her dress and went to her locker to try to open it again.

There was more to the story than some random act against an innocent girl, Ms. Morgan sensed. And whatever precipitated this cruel joke was the key to a Pandora's box that would probably be better off unopened.

"You can't leave the campus at this hour . . . and it would be well after midnight before your mother could get here."

"My godmother lives near here . . . in Dansville. That's only twenty minutes away. She can come pick me up with my mother's permission."

"Is that what you really want to do?"

Sherita was already in a sweatshirt and about to step into her jeans. Ms. Morgan picked her dress up off the floor and reached for a hanger. "We can get to the bottom of this you know."

"I don't want to talk about it, Ms. Morgan. Would you call my mother, please? I'll just tell her I had a great time and I feel like getting away for the weekend. She doesn't have to know anything else."

Ms. Morgan respected her wishes and obliged her request.

❧ ❧ ❧

The girls' perfumed fragrances were still potent, as fresh as their thoughts. They were rowdy and very much alive as they made their way up the stairs of Bryant Hall. Laughingly, they recounted one story after another about the night's events. Suite 210 was dark when they opened the door. Tyler hit the lights and was followed by Stephanie, Snoopy, and Princess.

"Where's Sherita?" Princess asked, noticing her unmade bed.

"I thought she was gonna show up with her mystery man," said Snoopy.

"Yeah, did you really?" asked Stephanie.

"I know my mouth almost dropped when Blair walked in with Zorley," said Princess.

"That was a bit crushing, wudn't it?" Tyler remarked. "I know Sherita thought Blair was her secret admirer."

"So where is she?" Snoopy questioned. "We haven't seen her all night."

In danced Saba, doing a freestyle two-step and carrying a strong residue of cigarette smoke on her. She and her friends had been feeling no pain all night. And the guy she was with put a smile on her face that none of them had seen before.

"Look at this," she stopped suddenly, passing Sherita's bed. She picked up a small portion of a damp hair weave and threw it to Stephanie.

"Must be Sherita's," Stephanie said, examining the track and throwing it over to Snoopy.

"Eww, get this thing out of here!" Snoopy squealed, slinging it over to Princess.

The glue on the track was still sticky, as if it hadn't been too long since its removal. "Something was goin' on up in here tonight. This is Sherita's hair," said Princess.

"Musta been a reason for her to take it out so soon like that," said Stephanie. "She just got her hair done earlier today."

An eerie feeling passed through the atmosphere, but everyone soon resumed their high spirits, talking and rehashing the fun of the event. They were into their T-shirts and pajamas, still reliving the Social when a startling knock came at the door.

"Girls, it's me," announced Ms. Morgan, peeping in, still wearing her evening dress. "I just wanted to let you know that Sherita wasn't feeling too well this evening, so her parents had someone come pick her up."

"Is she alright?" Stephanie asked.

"She'll be fine. Just needed to be home where she could be comfortable." Ms. Morgan's face was expressionless and her voice gave off no hint of trouble.

"She missed the party?" Snoopy asked.

"I . . . believe she did."

"But she was dressed and ready at the same time we were," recalled Princess. "And some of the girls said they saw her in the front of Founder's."

"If she came that far why wouldn't she come in?" Snoopy inquired.

"That's weird," said Saba, frowning.

"Yes it is, but I guess she just had a sudden change of heart," said Ms. Morgan. "It happens."

"That's too bad," Stephanie moaned, grabbing her pillow. "She missed a good time."

"Yes, she did." Ms. Morgan turned away to leave but then turned back with a half-smile emerging. "Princess, congratulations again, darling. We're proud of you."

"We *all* are," Stephanie said, leading the girls into applause.

"Okay, ladies, lights out at midnight."

When the door closed, Stephanie, Princess, and Snoopy launched into an episode of laughter.

Tyler and Saba looked at one another in confusion.

"Okay, right now I can use another smoke 'cause obviously I'm missing something." Saba opened her purse and put a cigarette in her mouth.

"You don't want to do that," warned Tyler.

"C'mon, it's not gonna kill anybody."

"She actually fell for it," said Stephanie, a sinister grin on her face. "But I thought she was gonna show up so we could have the pleasure. 'Cause I would've rubbed it all in her face."

"Stephanie, you really pulled it off!" Princess praised. For a brief second she felt remorse for having knowledge of the conspiracy. Her grandmother always spoke against seeking revenge. *When you try to do God's work, sometimes it comes back to bite you,* she'd say. Then Princess thought of what Sherita had done to her. *But don't provoke people, either. It was only a harmless little joke thought up by Stephanie to keep Sherita distracted. Shoot! She got off easy.*

"What the heck are y'all laughing about?" Saba asked, growing annoyed.

"Sherita deserved that and more," muttered Stephanie.

"Deserved what?" Tyler asked, sitting up in her bed.

"Just what came to her, that's what," replied Stephanie.

"Okay, what's the deal?" Saba demanded, holding her cigarette out of the window and lighting it.

"Want to know who the mystery date is?" said Stephanie in a soft, hushed tone. "It's a secret."

"Oh, come on, it's old now," Saba groaned. "What's the story?"

Stephanie, Snoopy, and Princess collapsed in laughter.

Slowly it dawned on her that a plot had occurred. "No, you didn't!"

"But you did!" Tyler retorted, throwing a pillow across the room into Stephanie's face. "You are cruel."

"No, no, we didn't," Stephanie surrendered. "We didn't, for real. But we might know who did."

"*Whoever* it was is cruel," said Tyler.

"Uh uh, she's the one that's cruel," Stephanie retorted. "If you knew what she did, you wouldn't be saying that."

"Really?" Tyler asked.

"Oh, girl, you don't know the half," Snoopy teased.

"Well, how come I wasn't let in on it?"

Saba inhaled three quick times, exhaled raggedly, and flicked the cigarette out of the window. "Forget all that, just tell us the details," she said, plopping down on Stephanie's bed. Tyler hurried over and together they sandwiched Stephanie and probed her for all the information. The story went on and on and so did the laughter. Past lights out, they were still talking to the sounds of Saturday R&B on the Quiet Storm.

Two lights remained on after they'd undressed and gone through their confessions. Saba turned the music down and was talking on her cell phone. Tyler studied the digital pictures that were taken during the evening and passed the camera over to Stephanie lying across from her.

"Next week this time I'll be home," Princess realized. She was still lying on Snoopy's bed, staring into the ceiling with the excitement of the evening still clinging to her. "Can't wait."

"You got a lot of friends at home?" asked Snoopy.

"Sort of . . . yeah. You're going home, too, right?"

"No, I think I'll stay here," Snoopy replied dismally and rolled over in the opposite direction.

"What about your friends at home?" Princess asked. "You have a lot of them?"

"No, I live in two different places, remember? I take turns between my mother and father, and I'm never in either place long enough to get to know anybody . . . unfortunately."

"Well . . . look at the bright side. Having two homes is not such a bad deal. Which one do you like better?"

"Can't really say which— My mom's house is a mansion and my father's is like . . . a museum. But, you know, she's a Taurus, he's a Virgo, and like . . . the stars just don't match. 'Cause when one—"

"You're livin' like that?" Princess asked, rejecting her astrological theories.

"Well, yeah, I guess."

"You come to Telham Park and see how the other half lives and there won't be no guessin'."

"Gladly," she responded. " 'Cause I'm always by myself."

Princess felt sympathy for the girl who had everything— except friends. "Why don't you take somebody home with you one weekend?" she suggested.

"What weekend is good for you?"

Princess chuckled, realizing the deliberate set-up. Snoopy wanted Princess to go home with her. More importantly, though, she wanted Princess to be her friend. Pleasant memories of unforgettable moments at Boravia flashed through Princess' mind. Snoopy was, in some way, a part of every one of them. She owed her at least a weekend, and even more. Besides, she could get a bird's-eye view of how the other half lived. "Hmm . . . let me think about it."

"Three weeks from today?"

"I shall *contemplate* that invitation."

"I'd love to visit New York," said Tyler.

"Really?"

"Yeah, and perhaps you could show us around."

"Since Saba lives there, too, we could all hang out."

"And Stephanie's right next door in Jersey," said Princess. "That would be nice."

Saba gave them a 'thumbs-up' in agreement, still talking on the phone.

Tyler sat up with a gleam in her eyes. "We could visit the Empire State Building, the Statue of Liberty, Greenwich Village . . . ooooh and Harlem."

"What do you know about Harlem?" Princess asked, exchanging glances with Snoopy and the Stephanie.

"Harlem is legendary. We hear of it in London all the time, especially about the soul food cuisine, and I would love to visit the Apollo."

"Uh oh." Princess was tickled by Tyler's enthusiasm. "So you want to do some 'Show Time,' see some history and chow down?"

"Yeah . . . I'd love to."

"I think that's do-able. We'll talk about it," Princess said and walked over to her bed, pulled the covers back and jumped in.

"Yo, yo, Stephanie. You goin' home tomorrow?" Saba asked, turning off her cell phone.

"Yep."

"I'm telling you now, you betta come in through the front door on Sunday. I don't do windows any more."

"Okay, now we're on the same page 'cause I don't need any more drama in my life," Snoopy agreed, turning off the switch of her bedside lamp.

"Cut out all that noise," said Stephanie, returning to her bed.

"Stephanie's gonna be a good girl from now on," Tyler said, turning off her camera and then the light.

Everybody soon retreated into their own world of dreams, but it was a long time before anyone slept.

From: "Princess Brixton"
To: "Nadira Watford"
Subject: Payback

Nadira,

You won't believe all the drama that's occurred here since I spoke with you. I feel like I've been thrust into a tornado and I'm still spinning. I can't give it all to you now, not good for the digestive system, but here's a little taste. The Millennium Social was a blast! It rained like cats and dogs, but it didn't matter. I was escorted in a stretch limo. That's right! I've got *tons of* pictures to show you. And guess who showed up? Lisa Capote, the girl who was attacked doing the Internet dating thing. She brought her father with her as her date and there wasn't a dry eye in the house. Then, when the presentations came they called my name to receive the Civic Award. It scared me like crazy. My feet were cemented to the floor and Terry had to move me to receive it.

But wait. Here's the 411 on my snakemate, I mean suitemate, Sherita. You know I like to stay clear of people once they show me who they really are. Well, people down here are not so forgiving. They believe in an "eye for an eye." When her plan with Terry failed she decided to sink her poison fangs into Blair. And let me tell you he's fine, plays on the team, and has rich parents. Blair starts teasing her right, you know with some small talk, and she gets beside herself. By the way, Terry is his boy and told him to do it. Then she starts receiving a rose every day for about ten days with this anonymous note, trying to make it seem all mysterious and everything. Before the event the hoochie was in seventh heaven, and she just knows they're from Blair. So on the night of the social she went all out, got this big weave thing going on, this red gown that was choking her and cost her mother a fortune. And believe me she thought she was a real 'Princess.'

But check it. Stephanie is out for revenge for the stunt she pulled trying to get her expelled so she gets one of Terry's friends to deliver the roses, but there is no secret admirer. To add some flavor to the mix Stephanie had arranged for her to receive a corsage. But she timed it to arrive at the door after everyone had already left. When she opened up the box and put it on her wrist there was a trick tube of invisible ink hidden along the edges of the corsage tape. It burst and smeared all over her hands. Then Blair brings this gorgeous honey to the social and we're waiting to see her face when they walk in but she never showed. Some students said they saw her, but she didn't come in. Well, she got an eyeful if she did.

When the social ended, we get back to the room; our houseparent tells us Sherita went home. A part of me feels sorry for her but she got off easy for what she had done. I don't expect we're gonna be having any more problems with her. Most people can't take what they dish out. On Terry, aside from his bad history with Sherita, he's a cool dude. Just can't see us as a twosome though, not now anyway. The whole thing left a bad taste in my mouth.

Can't wait to come home and see my people. Whew! I could use the rest. I'll be home by 6:30 on Friday. Let everybody know I'm coming. Peace.

LYLAS

thirteen

Miami June Stone dropped her last piece of Vuitton luggage on the floor, wondering how it would all fit in the small locker. Describing her former suitemates as "a lifeless sack of do nothings," she, too, was a disgruntled suitemate and was happy to move to Suite 210, replacing Sherita, who had requested a room change.

On an early June dawn in South Beach, Miami, a premature infant, was born to a very wealthy family. Drenched by the tropical Florida heat, she was a sun-bronzed strawberry blonde with sparkling emerald eyes.

"Ouch!" Miami June exclaimed, catching her finger in the locker while trying to close it.

"You got more stuff?" asked Snoopy, noticing another bag. "There's no way it's all gonna fit."

"I'll find a way," she said, picking up the smaller one. "My eyes are in there."

Stephanie watched her unpack the video cam. "A wee bit attached, aren't we?"

"Proof of life," she countered, smiling.

With her vivacious energy and curious nature, Miami June wanted to capture every significant moment of her existence at Boravia on camera, she told them. She said she wanted to look at the feature film of her life and see it amazingly unfold before her when she turns seventy.

NIGHTS WERE becoming longer for Princess and Thursday was no different. After reading the assigned chapter in her biology book for the second time, Princess lifted the remaining soil from underneath her fingernails with an aluminum file in even, semi-circular strokes. Digging for worms to dissect in biology class wasn't exactly her idea of a great day to write home about. Dissatisfied, she ran its point around the corners of her cuticles and removed other stubborn particles. No matter how many times she washed her hands, remnants of dirt remained in her fingernails.

Princess read long into the deep hours of the night when Boravia's campus was a serene haven, quiet and peaceful. Finding herself dozing, she turned off her night light and returned to her thoughts about going home. Anticipating the reunion of family and friends, stepping with the team, eating at McCuller's and sleeping in her own bed lulled her into sleep. Then, out of nowhere, in the universe of silence, came a strange sound like a sharp object running along a glass surface. She raised up in the darkness to determine its direction. No one else in the room budged. Moments later, the noise came again.

"Who's that?" said Snoopy, startled out of her sleep.

"I don't know and this is the second time I heard it," replied Princess.

"Stop playing, Stephanie," said Saba. On occasion she would run her nails along the wood on the side of her bed to try to scare them.

"Yeah, cut it out," said Tyler, rolling over. "I was already sleeping."

Slowly there came a low, gentle moan that slid into a husky groan. It was hardly a sound that would come from a girl, and one they'd never heard before.

"Stephanie," Saba called. "Stephanie!"

"Huh, what's the matter?" she replied, groggy.

"No, go this way," a heavy masculine voice said, belonging to none of them.

"What in the world?" Princess tossed her covers off and dashed toward the light.

The suitemates' eyes resisted the sudden burst of brightness. In that second of disorientation the voice rushed toward them, bolder this time. "Go this way."

"It's Miami!" Tyler exclaimed.

Their eyes leaped toward the tormented girl, struggling through what seemed to be a bad dream. "Go this way . . . this way." Then they heard a series of inaudible murmurs.

A supernatural air loomed over the room as they all stood still, stunned at what they were experiencing.

In another voice—smaller and dark—came words as clear as day: "The water is cold . . . too cold." Miami gasped frightfully and her body stiffened. "Too cold."

Fear overwhelmed Princess and she paced herself to breathe more easily, trying to avert the possibility of an asthma attack.

Miami began turning spasmodically from side to side, her loose hair sweeping over one side of her face to the other. A reddish hue appeared beneath her tanned skin. "I can see them coming. They're almost here. Come here!" she growled.

With a horrid shriek, Snoopy jumped out of bed and ran to the door.

"What's wrong with her?" Saba asked, her eyes rolling wildly.

"Is she sick?" Stephanie probed, crawling to the tip of her bed, gazing carefully.

"Maybe we should wake her?" Tyler suggested.

"But who is she?" Saba squealed.

Miami snorted. "Ten before four." Then she smacked her lips together several times. It was as if someone had inhabited her.

"Yo, she ain't playin'," Stephanie declared.

"Don't tell me this girl's got some crazy demon in her," said Snoopy, whose eyes were as big as golf balls.

"Expect me around midnight," a gravelly voice, louder and more sinister than the first one, bellowed. "It'll be a surprise." A diabolical laugh followed, sending the girls into a mad panic.

"Oh, my God!" Saba cried. She flew out of the bed so fast she rammed into Stephanie, causing them both to stumble and fall on the floor.

"Wait! Don't open the door and alarm everybody," Tyler urged, helping Stephanie and Saba to their feet. Breaking away from the frightened bunch, she daringly walked over to Miami. "I think she's sleeping," she observed, mystified.

Princess, Saba, Stephanie and Snoopy huddled together at the door like scared little chickens waiting to break out at any second.

Tyler gently shook her. "Miami, wake up. Miami." Unexpectedly, she opened her eyes. In staunch surprise, the girls simultaneously gasped.

"What's the matter?" asked Miami in her normal voice, sounding tired and sleepy.

"You okay?" questioned Tyler.

"Yeah . . . what's goin' on?" Miami's green eyes looked like little rubies drowning in a red-rimmed sea and they wandered over to the girls at the door. "What are y'all doing?" she asked, looking at them in total confusion.

Unutterable awe held the girls' words hostage.

"What happened to you?" Tyler wanted to know.

"What do you mean, I was sleeping."

The girls gazed at her, horrified, afraid to move.

"What is it, guys? You look like you saw a ghost."

"Www . . . we did," stuttered Snoopy.

"Who are you?" Saba queried desperately.

"What kind of question is that?" Miami sat up and pushed her hair away from her face.

Saba's summary of what had happened was as surprising to Miami as it was to the rest of them. As the girls talked, and much of their fear dissipated, they returned to their beds. The question, however, still remained in their minds. What were those strange masculine voices coming out of this petite girl? Sleep didn't come easily for anyone in the few hours that remained before dawn.

"IF THERE'S no traffic they should be here in about an hour," Princess replied, watching Stephanie style her hair. "You should wear your hair like that when you're competing. Dudes will be chasing you for real and then Damien—"

"C'mon, we've got just enough time," said Stephanie, grabbing Princess and then shooting out the door. "They're out of here in twenty minutes. Let's go!"

Like other Boravian Warrior fans, Princess, Stephanie, Miami, and Snoopy went out to extend their well wishes to the basketball team for the weekend's game at Exelior Academy in Upstate New York.

Friday afternoon was slowly slipping into evening, bringing with it nippy winds. "Freedom!" shouted Stephanie, smacking the hands of one of her classmates driving off the grounds. Boravians had changed into their street clothes, suitcases were lined up outside, cell phone chatter was ablaze, and iPods were at their sides. Many students had already left for the weekend.

By now the girls had forgiven Miami June for the stunt she had pulled, imitating the characters of the boys who had drowned back in the early twentieth century. They discovered her video cam positioned for filming on her nightstand the next morning. Tyler suspected something foul and forced her to rewind it. Caught cold, she had to admit that she was testing her drama skills and the best way to critique her work was to capture herself on film in action with a live audience. She said she was preparing herself for Hollywood—and believed it with all her heart.

As far as the girls were concerned, she was well on her way.

THE BORAVIA Warriors loaded up their overnight bags, one by one, in the storage compartment on the side of the bus. The girls made their way through the crowd of spectators to get closer to them.

Spotting Princess, Terry vigorously cut through throngs of people to get to her. "Whas poppin?" he asked, embracing her. "I knew you weren't gonna let me leave without saying good-bye. You alright?"

"I'm good. You ready?"

"Ready to win, baby."

"Look," Princess said, turning her face to the right. She was wearing Terry's earring. "It'll keep you safe . . . and hopefully bring you some good luck."

Terry pulled her toward him. As he was reminded of her generous curves, he leaned into her and whispered, "Why don't you stop playin'. You know you belong to me . . . and I'ma gitchu!"

Princess relaxed her smile, gazed into his melting eyes and said, "Keep dreamin'."

Terry laughed out loud. "You know I will. A brother ain't got no ego when it comes to gettin' what he wants. I'm gonna dream 'til I can't dream no mo'," he bellowed, and then hugged her again. "So whatcha gonna do while I'm gone?"

"We're gonna get something to eat right now and kill some time. My family is on their way to pick me up."

Terry eyed Princess lovingly, the wind aggressively sweeping his face. "Don't be goin' home teasing those little boys in Telham Park. I don't wanna hear nothing when I come back." Terry spoke as if he was the only one in Princess' heart. Just then he was interrupted by a teammate, but quietly returned back to their conversation.

"Ay, you know somethin'?"

"What?"

"That wasn't no accident when I ran into you in the hall on your first day here. I was looking for you."

Taken aback, Princess shot him a puzzled glance. "You didn't even know me," she said, glancing at the people around them. Stephanie and Damien were not far from them, holding on closely to one another.

"No, see, first I got curious about your name," Terry reminisced, nodding coolly. "I saw your information when they were putting your orientation package together in Mr. Quinn's office. I figured you were my people because of your address, but I wasn't really sure. When I saw you in the hallway that first day, I knew I wanted to meet you."

"You serious?"

"Just as serious as I am about wantin' to kiss those juicy lips of yours, right now, this very second."

"You're crazy, git outta here!"

"Warriors, time to move," commanded Coach Myerson.

Terry dropped Princess' hand, cupped her face and pressed his lips against hers. "I bet your boys at home can't do that."

Princess' timid smile was a tacit acknowledgment of the truth. "Have a good time . . . and bring back a trophy, okay."

"I will, just for you."

A part of Princess wanted an encore of their kiss, and Terry knew it. She looked off into the sun, avoiding his eyes while he watched the last few members of the team board the bus.

"We're moving out, let's go," said Coach Myerson.

Terry pulled her within his embrace, giving her a big hug, a quick kiss to the cheek, and proceeded to walk away. Before he reached the bus he abruptly stopped, turned back and winked. "Be good, girl."

ABOUT THE AUTHOR

JENNIFER BURTON, a native of New York City, has always been intrigued with multicultural interaction. While teaching in a Brooklyn high school, she became deeply steeped in youth culture, observing their enthusiasm for urban contemporary fiction. Her literary insight, along with her passion for writing, prompted the creation of the Telham Park series. Jennifer resides in New Jersey.